The Camera Never Lies

Center Point
Large Print

Also by David Rawlings and available from Center Point Large Print:

The Baggage Handler

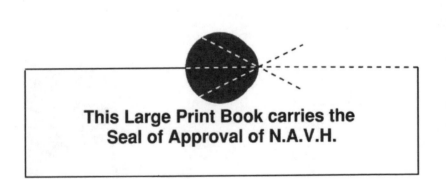

This Large Print Book carries the Seal of Approval of N.A.V.H.

The Camera Never Lies

a novel

DAVID RAWLINGS

CENTER POINT LARGE PRINT
THORNDIKE, MAINE

This Center Point Large Print edition
is published in the year 2020 by arrangement with
Thomas Nelson.

The text of this Large Print edition is unabridged.
In other aspects, this book may vary
from the original edition.
Printed in the United States of America
on permanent paper.
Set in 16-point Times New Roman type.

ISBN: 978-1-64358-464-5

The Library of Congress has cataloged this record
under Library of Congress Control Number: 2019950857

What would you do if your secrets were revealed to those around you?

One

Eighty-eight years of life reduced to a vintage, cracked briefcase sat before Daniel Whiteley. Gramps used to joke he loved this briefcase because it matched his complexion—weathered and beaten, knocked around at the edges. A survivor.

But now Gramps was gone.

The dusty leather contained not his soul but his meager possessions, entombed by rust-seized locks in an arthritic grip. Daniel stared at what remained of his grandfather and sipped at his watery, soulless coffee.

His mother wiped away a tear. "He was adamant I give it to you straight after the funeral."

As if he were the only thing holding her up, she dissolved into Daniel's embrace, and he raised his Styrofoam cup as she stifled a sob into his chest. Then she stepped back, pressing the creases from her shapeless black dress to distract another wave of emotion. "You spoke so well. He would have been proud of you."

"It was important I got it right." So important he'd worn a tie for the first time in years. He wouldn't let down his hero.

He clasped the briefcase handle and lifted it, feeling an unexpected weight.

"You look so much like him." Emotion swallowed his mother's sentence, and she dabbed at her eyes with a sodden handkerchief. "Where's Kelly?"

"Had to go back to work."

The tiniest frown tugged at the corner of her mouth. "How is Milly after the funeral?"

Daniel looked over his mother's head to the top of his daughter's, her gaze buried in her phone. She fidgeted on the last plastic chair in the row against the wall of the tiny room of the funeral home that only thirty minutes earlier had been half filled with people who had gathered to bid farewell to Gramps.

"She's quiet, but that's just a normal grief reaction." But he knew it was more than that. Milly was becoming a puzzle not even his master's degree in counseling could solve. She was twelve years old now, a time of life when a father's pride and dread should emerge in equal measure. The testing of boundaries for independence. A whole universe of dribbling, hormone-infected boys. Exploring the edges of the fun the world had to offer. But instead his daughter was growing quieter by the day.

"And Kelly?"

"It's hard to say. She's sad about Gramps, but she won't accept my help to work through anything she's dealing with."

"Is that why you aren't taking the rest of the day off to spend with your family?"

"Three of my afternoon appointments are new

8

couples, so no. Thanks for looking after Milly."

His mother reached up, a familiar stroke of his cheek. "I'm so proud of what you've achieved, especially with your book."

No Secrets was the difference between just staying afloat and living in luxury on the cliff tops in his late thirties. He was so fortunate to have stumbled across the idea for the book.

"I want you to be happy, Daniel."

He fobbed her off with a side hug. This was not the time to have *that* conversation. "Thanks, Mom. I'll call you tomorrow so we can work out a time to go through the last of Gramps's stuff."

His mother deposited the sodden handkerchief in her oversized handbag and then drew out an envelope with trembling fingers.

"There's one more thing. He wanted you to have this." She glanced again at the familiar writing, and the tears returned. "I need to talk to the funeral director—" Another cresting wave of emotion carried her from the room.

The last of Gramps sat at Daniel's feet, his last words in his hands. He took another lukewarm sip as he studied the envelope and the two words printed across the front in a stilted hand.

For Daniel

He drained the Styrofoam cup, ran a finger under the sealed flap, and drew out a single page filled with Gramps's upright handwriting. He ran a hand through his thick black curls and then adjusted his glasses as the sadness, clamped down for the funeral, wriggled free. For the last time, Gramps spoke to him.

My boy, you often told me very little surprises you, so I thought I would speak to you from beyond the grave. I'm sure that might.

Daniel chuckled as the gravel in Gramps's voice echoed in his head and shook loose a tear.

I'm so proud of the man you've become, with the success of your counseling practice and, of course, that book.

Daniel smiled through a bitten lip and filmed eyes.

I know you've got great insights into other people, but I worry for your family, Daniel. When I've raised this before, you've always shifted the conversation. Forgive an old man for advising the counselor, but I can see where your hearts are and where you're headed. Based on your current trajectory, I'm not sure you'll last.

Daniel winced as he sucked in a breath. He looked across to his distant daughter, thumbs hammering at her phone, within reach yet so far away.

I can help. I'm leaving you this gift I wish I had in my younger days, when choices in front of me were easier and would have saved so much pain.

The briefcase sat at his feet. Its leather shone in patches, and cracks on the lid revealed a paisley pattern beneath. Silver corners were burnished and tarnished, and combination tumblers with faded numbers sat on either side of the clasps.

My gift to you is in my old briefcase. I'm sure you'll be able to unlock it. The combination represents the most special day in my life.

The first tear fell onto the quivering page as Daniel read the final words Gramps would ever say to him.

I never allowed you to touch it, but you need it now. I have left it for you and not your mother because I know you need its truth. Please use it wisely; it has freed me from so much and taught me there's

11

always more to life than what we see. I love you.

Gramps

The gravel died away, and Gramps became silent in Daniel's life.

More tears came—a normal grief reaction—as he reached for the briefcase. *The most special day in my life.* Daniel chuckled to himself. He'd heard that phrase every year just before he blew out the candles. On the first lock, 0–1–1. On the other, 7–8–3.

His birthday.

The locks snapped open with a *thunk.* A puff of nostalgia and Old Spice drifted out as Daniel lifted the lid to find the one thing in Gramps's life he was never allowed to share.

His old Olympus camera.

Heavy, black and silver—from a time when the camera pointed away from photographers and not back at them while they made a face like a duck.

Daniel lifted it out with reverence; it was a sacred relic. He ran his thumb across the thick knobs and stiff levers, surrounded by tiny etched numbers. A rising sense of the forbidden grabbed him as his finger rested on the trigger where Gramps's weathered and lined index finger had once sat.

Daniel squinted through the viewfinder, and the tiny room came alive. The fading plastic chairs sparkled like new. The fluorescent lighting was somehow more yellow, more natural. Milly hunched even further over her phone. He brushed a roughness on the bottom of the camera and flipped it over to find an inscription in an elegant cursive script.

No matter what you think you might see, the camera never lies.

Gramps could be melodramatic when he wanted to be.

Film was already in the camera. That was good; he had no idea where he'd buy any.

Something else was in the briefcase—a flash of red. Daniel pulled out a small book with a fading red cover and a word stenciled on the front in worn gold: Photos. He felt another rising sense of the forbidden; he had seen few of Gramps's photos and never this album.

The book creaked open with a stiff groan. On each page was a single photograph held in place with tiny black triangles—Daniel recognized two of Gramps's friends from the funeral. The color in the photos was washed out, as if someone had dialed it down when the photos were processed.

As he flipped the pages, he noticed something odd about the photographs. Unsmiling eyes looked everywhere but at the camera. It was as if they'd been taken the split second before the subject knew the camera was there. One of Gramps's friends—a man in his sixties who had delivered a reading at the funeral—lunged to block a computer screen with his hand. Another friend; the curl of cigarette smoke emerged from behind her back.

These photos were poor quality and embarrassing. Why put them in an album?

Daniel turned another page. There was Gramps's friend Garth, a gray woolen beanie jammed down on escaping wisps of gray hair, a bushy unkempt beard, punctuated by a pained grin full of teeth that looked like a vandalized graveyard. He leaned against a shuttered door in a bleak back alley, forlorn eyes pleading with the night sky. But Garth had spoken at the funeral, clean-shaven and resplendent in a striped woolen vest and crisp white shirt. Daniel was sure he didn't live on the streets.

Another page. Gramps sat in his beloved burgundy recliner—although it was now a dull, dirty pink—smiling as he tore up a betting slip. A sad revelation washed over Daniel as the pieces locked into place. He often quizzed Gramps on his lack of money and meager possessions, and now he knew why. Gramps never mentioned he was a gambler. But why get someone to take a photo of it?

Another page, and his own face appeared, pain and frustration on display in crisp color. He sat at one end of the couch in his expansive living room, tight arms folded across his chest, white and pink balloons floating at his shoulder. Kelly sat at the other end of the couch, overdressed for a child's party, blond hair styled to perfection. As usual. Under her outstretched painted nails was . . . a pill bottle? It sat on a sheet of paper as Kelly threw a furtive glance over her shoulder at him, her brown eyes wide.

On the next page of the tiny album, the same photo. Why would Gramps have two copies? But no, this one was different. While Kelly's fingers still splayed over white plastic, in this one Daniel's face beamed at someone off camera, his anger gone. Daniel's professional radar pinged. He should have been seen enjoying his own daughter's birthday party, not fuming at his wife while happy to see other people. He prided himself on his poker face. It was a professional necessity when a conga line of excuses rolled out from the couples who sat opposite him on the couch in his office, giving lame reasons for selfish choices or justifications to wallpaper over guilt. Before he advised them that the best thing to do was to be honest with each other and keep no secrets.

Daniel stared harder at the plastic under Kelly's fingers. Why would she be holding a bottle of pills at Milly's birthday party? Something was up. He'd spent enough time sitting five feet from people who tried—and failed—to hide things from their partner and his probing questions.

He'd have to ask her what was going on. Again. He hoped it would go better this time.

The stiff spine creaked as Daniel reached the final photo, only halfway through this strange album. Another familiar face. Milly sat on a chair in the corner of their living room in her new dress, which she had spent hours choosing to match the pink-and-white theme she'd set for her twelfth birthday party. Her eyes lowered, hands clasped on her lap, the camera flash catching the trickle of a tear down her cheek.

This time embarrassment didn't flood through Daniel. It was guilt. Their rush to cater to everyone else at the party meant he didn't notice Milly at all, and he should have. The pulse of his family had quickened because of their busyness, but it had not brought life.

He looked up at Milly, still head down over her device in an almost mirror image of the photo he held in his hand. Daniel sighed hard. It was another reminder that for all the families he'd saved as a counselor, his own was in danger of falling apart.

Two

The traffic ahead of Kelly smeared into a kaleidoscope of taillights and vague color on bumpers.

Tears will do that.

Kelly drummed them away to music on the steering wheel as she drove from the funeral. Away from her family. She had ten minutes until she called on a new children's clinic and rolled out the usual spiel about the wonder drug ridding families of frustration all over the city. She should be home, not going back to work after a funeral. But this was one more time when the choice was taken from her. As she shot through traffic, Kelly checked the rearview mirror and tried a smile. Sadness still lurked. That would have to go. You only got one chance to make a good first impression, and that didn't happen with red, puffy eyes.

Gramps's passing would leave a big hole in her life. A caring man with a kind word to say—and he always knew the right time to say it. He was almost her grandfather, too, and he was the one who could get through to Daniel.

The next song from the radio eased into the car—plaintive piano chords in a careful tread over rising violins. The tears crept forward, and Kelly punched for another station. Jagged synth chords backed with the attitude of an all-girl group banished her tears with a finger snap.

The further apart she and Daniel drifted, the more he gravitated toward work. He only talked about people at the practice—the brilliant Anna, whom she had tagged his work-wife out of frustration, or that new receptionist with blouses always two sizes too small.

On the on-ramp to the freeway, the traffic thinned, and she put down her foot. The concrete ribbon stretched into the distance, dry, empty plains shepherding it to the horizon.

Her fingers drummed again as the music powered on. They hadn't had bad times; their good times were just in the rearview mirror. Their early days were a soaring mountain range— the peaks of joy and the valleys of conflict that always rose to another peak. Always. But they had hit the flats.

The tears welled again. A failed wife. That's what she felt like.

Marriage counseling had given her the house of her dreams on the cliffs, but it came with a steep price: more of their conversations devolved into pseudo appointments. Daniel couldn't help but put on his professional hat. Why couldn't he just *be* in his own marriage instead of diagnosing it? She wanted to talk with the old Daniel—her husband and not the go-to counselor who fixed people. They had spent more than a decade talking about anything and everything, but now the only safe topic of discussion was ferrying Milly around.

Milly.

Her daughter who each day took a step away from her as she disappeared into herself. Kelly had read every parenting book she could. There had to be more to Milly than the first seeds of teenage rebellion. It looked more like a quiet resignation as if accepting a sad inevitability.

A failing mother. That's what she felt like.

Kelly left the freeway as the song ended abruptly on aggressive three-part harmony and made way for softer piano. She shut off the radio. Another quick glance in the rearview mirror, and she blinked hard to clear her eyes as she threaded her way through suburban traffic.

Just another few months.

Giving the "110 percent" required of her at work was more than impossible when her heart was somewhere else. In the excitement of receiving the advance from Daniel's publisher, they'd bought the house on Clifftop Drive. Her dream home, with a kitchen big enough to start her own catering business, had been bought on a promise—his second book being a bestseller too. But it was taking Daniel far longer to write it than he said it would. Longer than she needed.

So she'd taken the job offered through her best friend. At least she would be helping people— families in particular. At least it was that way at the start.

Just another few months. But Milly didn't need her in a few months. She needed her now.

Kelly swung into a parking lot, her car sputtering a little as if cringing in the company of Audis and BMWs. She reached across the seat and grabbed her sample bag emblazoned with Rubicon Pharma. Branded, like all cattle were.

Kelly pulled down her sun visor to look into its mirror. As she dabbed at runaway mascara, she tried her best customer-service smile. It sagged under the grief of the day and placed another brick in her wall of resentment toward work. More than anything, she wanted to draw a big line through that day's calendar square, to hold Milly, to be held by Daniel. But the choice wasn't hers. In so many ways.

Gramps burst back into her thinking, regaling her with the importance of honesty—a crusade he'd championed in the final year of his life. His gentle voice, firm but insistent: *The truth will set you free.* And in those last few months, he had said things to her—things with such clarity— that she wondered where he was getting his information. Whispered secrets with Daniel out of the room, based in truth she dared not speak aloud.

The lid on her emotions bubbled as more tears welled.

With a deep sigh, Kelly pasted a smile on her face as she strode toward the clinic, the doors gliding open as she ran through the script in her head. The script that would promise a wonder drug for grateful parents losing the battle against a tiny screen for their child's hands.

A script that was getting harder to deliver and impossible to believe in.

Three

The woman shook her frazzled brunette locks in disbelief as she clung to one end of the couch in Daniel's office. Crammed into the other end—across pristine leather in the middle section on which no one ever sat—was a balding, broad-shouldered man bursting out of a tight polo shirt, wringing rough hands, and staring at the carpet.

Two sofa chairs sat unoccupied, and Daniel smiled. Mark and Laurie Wood might be far apart, but they were still together. A good sign. Couples who chose the single chairs came to him far too late.

Mark gave his halting take on a stalled marriage to the carpet. "To answer your question, things have changed."

Daniel made another note, although he might as well have ticked a box. He heard that every day. The spark that brought this couple together had faded like their framed wedding photograph after years in the afternoon sun. He looked at the frames on his desk, captured moments of family happiness, his credibility to new couples. Gramps's camera sat waiting for the last few minutes of this final appointment of the day to tick over.

Mark's hesitant words tripped over one another on their way out, his uneasy confidence rising. "We do whatever's next on the calendar. It's not that we've moved on to someone else—at least I haven't." Then a quick sideways glance to catch a reaction confirming long-held suspicions.

The brunette locks shook again.

A thought tapped in a quiet corner of Daniel's mind. A familiarity. A feeling too close for comfort.

The skin on Mark's rough, red hands was now striped with white. "I'm not sure how to say it—" Mark's forty-five-minute silence cracked as his words tumbled out. Laurie squirmed on the sofa, keen to contribute, to clarify and correct. Mark looked up, sheepish embarrassment on his face. "What's that saying? Like ships passing in the night? That's us."

The thought tapped again. Daniel's jeans rustled as he shifted his weight to usher it to one side. "Thank you for your openness and honesty, Mark." He sat with fingers steepled under his nose. "May I give you my take on where you are?"

Laurie leaned forward with an expectant nod, no doubt hopeful of an immediate solution to the pain of their marital struggle. "Please."

"I don't think it's ships passing in the night. You're sailing alone and don't even know another ship is sailing alongside you."

Laurie reached for the tissue box on the coffee table.

The familiarity tapped again.

"You need to bring some things out into the open. You each hold a part of the solution." Daniel spread his hands at the expected response.

Two sets of defenses shot up with a *clunk*. Mark resumed the hand-wringing, and Laurie leaned deeper into the couch.

"I won't tell you to share everything this minute, but the first step is a willingness to consider it."

He reached to the neat stack of white-spined books on his desk and handed one to each of them. "You might have seen my book."

Laurie snatched it and resumed her nodding—they were in his office because she'd seen Daniel on TV promoting *No Secrets*. All the new couples said that. His book wasn't just a bestseller; it had lifted the practice out of near bankruptcy after Howard, his mentor and boss who had established Crossroads Counseling, passed away.

Mark studied the book's spine, inspecting its construction.

Laurie pored over the opening pages. "All my girlfriends have said it's as if you've put a lifetime's worth of knowledge into it."

Mark continued to study the book, its cover closed.

Daniel leaned forward with a conspiratorial

whisper. "I've also got an audiobook version if you're not much into reading."

Mark smiled in relief as the men in Daniel's office often did when given the chance to *not* read something.

Laurie's eyes seemed to devour page after page, searching for the solution to her broken marriage.

Daniel studied the couple. Mark's distance from the solution to their problem. Laurie's overeager expectation of a quick fix. "I'm not giving this to you because it's *my* book. I'm giving it to you because I believe this is what you need. No secrets. Honesty is the key to your marriage recovering and then thriving."

His desk phone buzzed. "Let's leave it there today. Please read the book, and for our next session, we'll work toward taking that first step in your being honest with each other."

Mark and Laurie stood as one. Another good sign.

"Monique will look after your next appointment." Daniel ushered them from his office and then flopped back into his chair. The Woods were another couple who had buried their differences deep enough to be out of reach but shallow enough so they both knew they were there. He heard the same thing every day from couples who poured through his office door as if the community were a clown car of unhappy relationships.

Daniel picked up Gramps's camera. His professional day over, the moment had arrived. He lifted the gift to his eye, and when he spun his chair, luscious blond tresses filled his vision, along with a ruby-red smile. His welcome to work every morning for the past month.

Monique gave a playful rap on the door. "May I speak to you for a moment, Daniel?"

With a broad smile, Daniel put down the camera. "Of course."

She bounced into his office, a heady mix of youthful energy and perfume. She perched on the edge of the couch, her long legs crossed as she held out a small gift box tied with an extravagant red ribbon. "I just wanted to say I'm sorry for your loss."

Daniel was touched. She was sweet, and everyone loved her youthful enthusiasm. "Thanks, Monique. That's special."

He tugged on the ribbon, and a flash caught his eye as he lifted the lid of the box. Gold. Two cuff links nestled in pristine white silk. Two engraved letters on each. His initials.

Daniel stopped, unsure how to address a gift so over-the-top. She couldn't afford to give it, and he couldn't afford to receive it.

Monique caught his hesitation, and her smile dimmed. "You looked so sad when you told me how much your Gramps meant to you."

He evaluated his options like a world-class

Rubik's Cube champion, flicking through responses to find the right ones. The wrong choice could crush her. Or him. "Monique . . . uh . . . this gift is . . ."

Her voice quickened. "You mentioned on my third day here that cuff links are smart."

The box held only two small pins. Where was the harm in that?

Monique beamed as he pulled back his suit jacket and put them on, and then she pointed to the photograph on his desk. "Is that Gramps?"

Daniel reached past the smiling family photo to grab the frame that held his younger self with the older man, hair graying around his temples and flowing behind him. A hippie stuck in time.

"No, that was old Howard Jones. He started this practice and brought me in fresh from earning my master's. He gave me a gift I've shared with many people since. He's been gone three years."

Monique's eyes sparkled, almost reflecting the sheen on her lips. "I'm so glad I'm now part of your team. We help a lot of people."

"It's great to have you on board, Monique. You're a terrific addition to the Crossroads family." Daniel settled into the conversation. It was nice to talk without scanning for an agenda behind any given sentence.

Monique reached across for another photo frame, showing Daniel in the middle of a group of schoolchildren. A waft of perfume followed her. "Is this the school counseling program?"

The photo represented Daniel's contribution to Milly's school, to assuage the guilt from not having time for hockey practice or mind-numbing school board meetings. Free counseling for at-risk youth.

Her blond tresses bounced inches from Daniel's nose as she ran a finger across the photograph. "You give so much of yourself." Her milk-chocolate eyes connected with him over the top of the frame. "Considering that, who looks after you?"

The base of Daniel's spine tingled, a long-lost memory of teenage days and the thrill of the chase.

From the corridor a phone rang, and Monique touched her Bluetooth headset. "Welcome to Crossroads Counseling!"

A polite knock at the door was followed by a brunette head with a burgundy streak in defiance of early gray.

Monique's fingers twinkled as she sashayed out the door. "There's a waiting list to see Mr. Whiteley, but . . ."

The owner of the burgundy streak took a seat and studied him. Anna Potts—Howard's second recruit. "How are you after the funeral, Boss?"

"Good. I held it together during my eulogy—just. And we've talked about this Boss label."

Anna grinned. "I'm sure it will be no surprise

when I tell you it's okay to let out your feelings." She eyed the empty gift box and then the flash of gold on his sleeve. She raised an eyebrow. "Nice cuff links."

There was no point defending the gift. A towering intellect packed into a slight frame, Anna had only to hoist an eyebrow and you crumbled.

"You know how we talked about having each other's back at the office?"

It was clear what was coming.

"You should be careful with Monique's attention."

Daniel fought the urge to squirm in his seat, a reversal of the usual dynamic in this office. "Look, it's innocent, and she's naive. There's nothing to it."

The eyebrow stayed up. "Would you mention that gift to Kelly?"

Daniel exhaled through clenched teeth. "I'll tell her tonight."

Anna offered him a warm smile. Her natural smile, not the one a counselor saves for clients in the middle of a "don't blame me" story. "I'm not saying it will go well, but you are the *No Secrets* guy, right?"

She *was* right. As always. "You know me better than anyone, don't you?"

"We've worked together for years, Daniel. And at Milly's birthday party, I saw Kelly corner you in the kitchen about talking to that gorgeous woman in the red dress. We all did."

Daniel shook the memory from his head—the pleasant chat with another parent from school until Kelly had hovered like a government drone checking the perimeter.

"And if my husband came home with new jewelry without an explanation, my senses would be on high alert. Anyway, I didn't come in here for a counseling session. I've had an idea. We've had our thousandth client case since you took over from Howard, so we should celebrate. And it would be nice for you to focus on something positive after you've lost Gramps."

Celebrating *was* a good idea—one Daniel had often suggested but not considered for himself. It was nice for someone to notice. That was the problem when you resolved other people's issues twenty-four hours a day. Other people didn't realize you had them too.

"Daniel, you've done amazing things since Howard passed the baton."

"*We* have, and maybe we could hold this celebration at our home. Kelly would love to cater, I'm sure."

Anna smirked. "You think she'll be okay with us in her home?"

"She's got nothing to be jealous about."

"*We* both know that, but *she* doesn't seem to. She hasn't been subtle in the past."

Another knock at the door. "I hear the funeral went well."

Daniel gestured in a tall man who could have stepped from the pages of a fashion magazine—sharp lines over casual blue. Peter Gardner was a great counselor and an asset to Daniel in so many ways.

"It did. Thanks, Peter. End of an era, glad to have closure."

Peter looked first over one shoulder, then over the other, and then back at Daniel. "Are you talking to me? I'm a friend *and* a counselor. You don't need to put that on."

Monique leaned into the room, took one look at the flash of gold on Daniel's cuffs, and beamed. "Anna, your four o'clock is here."

Anna made her way to the door, jerking her head in the direction of Monique's grin. *See?* Daniel nodded in return.

Peter pointed to the camera on his desk and whistled. "That's a beautiful thing."

Daniel handed it over. "I thought you'd like to see it. It belonged to Gramps, and he left it to me."

Peter held it up to his eye. "Great camera—I've had two Olympuses myself." He inspected the badge on the front. "The Infinity model. Can't say I've heard of that one before, and I know everything about the Olympus range." He read the inscription aloud. " 'The camera never lies'—well, that's true."

"I can't wait to use it. I haven't yet had a chance to even look at it."

Peter flipped the camera around and checked the tiny window on the back. "Someone has. There aren't any shots left on this film."

Four

The scrape of forks on dinner plates echoed through a dining area that could fit ten but felt too small for the three of them. The grandfather clock counted out steady measures of silence, marking the groaning distance between each snatch of conversation.

Kelly chewed on a hunk of steak as she studied Milly, who parted the curtains of her hair with mouthfuls of food. Kelly hoped Gramps's passing would bridge the gap between them for a moment, so they could go back to that time when Milly came running from anywhere in the house when she heard Daniel's key in the front door. So would she.

"I thought today was a lovely farewell to Gramps." Kelly laid the first plank in that bridge.

Milly gave the smallest nod and shared a sad smile from below her fringe. "He would have liked seeing people come to say good-bye." She resumed pushing vegetables around her plate, and the room again filled with ticking.

Daniel brushed his mouth with a napkin. "How are you after saying good-bye to him today, Mill?"

"I said good-bye before he died." She lowered sad eyes again.

Kelly's heart burst with the sputtering connection, but at least it was better than no conversation at all. "Your poem was truly beautiful." She left a gap in the conversation for Milly to fill.

Tick . . . tick . . . tick . . .

Instead, Daniel kept the conversational ball in the air with a goofy smile. The one she fell in love with. "I was so proud of you."

Forks resumed their scraping. Kelly threw a glance at Daniel, who was now studying his daughter, eyes narrowed, brow knotted. Her husband's professional hat was on.

"Perhaps we should remember happier times. Did you have fun at your birthday party, Mill?"

Milly's fork halted, and the sad smile on her lips hardened.

Kelly frowned at Daniel. *What are you talking about?*

Tick . . . tick . . . tick . . .

Daniel shook his head at Milly's silence and turned back to Kelly. "How was the appointment with the clinic?"

Kelly filled her glass. "Another day, another promise that Rubicon Pharma has the drugs to fix anything."

Tick . . . tick . . . tick . . .

"So you're losing faith in the healing powers of Mendacium?"

Kelly sawed at her steak, the tension from Daniel's usual quip about quick-fix medication driving her hand like a piston. "It's great to see families helped. That's one reason I liked this job in the first place. It just seems that the focus is more on the fix, not the family."

Daniel chuckled. "That sounds like any first appointment with a couple."

Tick . . . tick . . . tick . . .

The silence descended again, and Daniel resumed his study of Milly.

Kelly watched the two most important people in her life in a silent marionette display. Her heart sank, along with the hope they could shake off this heavy tension. Placing her cell phone on the table, she raised a white flag to the hope of a deeper conversation and headed to familiar ground. "We should organize the rest of the week now that the funeral is out of the way." The tension eased as they coordinated appointments, school, and work like air traffic controllers juggling a fleet of aircraft.

Kelly kept Milly in the corner of her eye. Her brows loosened as the conversation moved to the logistics of dance lessons and Homework Club. She even contributed a full sentence. Sometimes two.

Daniel placed his cutlery on his now-empty

plate. "Hey, Mill, did any of your friends ever mention the great time they had at your birthday party?"

Kelly almost dropped her glass. Why was he pressing on this?

Milly's mask was back, fixed in place by her knotted brow. "Why?"

Kelly tensed as Daniel leaned forward on his elbows. He had done everything but ask his daughter to lie down on a couch in his office. "We haven't talked about it—with Gramps and everything—so I wanted to check in with you."

The soft chime of the half hour floated out from the grandfather clock before it resumed its tutting.

"Because it's hard to know if people have had a good time when you're busy catering to everyone else—"

With a heavy sigh, Milly pushed away her plate and left the table, dragging her feet up the stairs.

Kelly's grief bubbled to the surface in a wash with every other emotion she'd held back all afternoon. "What on earth was all that about?"

Daniel turned to her. "I thought I'd try another angle to work out what's wrong with her."

"Work out what's wrong with her? We just buried Gramps! Why do you have to be a professional all the time? She doesn't need you to be a counselor. She needs you to be her father."

Daniel moved to answer, but stopped, catching his words before they came out.

Kelly continued. "All she needs is *us* at the moment. In fact, she needs *me* at home."

Daniel rolled his eyes. "That conversation again. It's only another couple of months until I can get the next book written. And to be honest, if you're referring to something else, it's better for us to have things out in the open with no secrets—"

Kelly leaped to her feet, plates and utensils crashing together as she snatched them from the table. "Now you're doing it to me." She stormed over to the kitchen sink. The entire house seemed to echo with the harsh wash of pounding water against polished stainless steel.

"I'm sorry, okay? I found out something today that could be the reason for her withdrawal, so I wanted to—"

Water flicked from the sink with Kelly's intense rinsing. "You push her away every time you try to fix her." She flung open the dishwasher door.

As Daniel placed glasses next to the sink, Kelly saw the flash of gold on his shirt cuffs. They were new.

"As I was about to say, I found out something today that might explain why she's so down. A photo from her birthday party."

Kelly's scrubbing slowed. "What photo?"

Daniel raised a finger and headed toward

his study, returning with an old briefcase. He placed it on the kitchen counter, thumbed in a combination, and popped open the clasps with a *thunk*. The smell of Old Spice wafted toward Kelly, waking memories of Gramps, as Daniel pulled out a small book. The pages groaned as Daniel flicked through them, before he held the book open for her to see. "Do you remember that?"

The pain she felt was like a knife slicing deep into her heart. Her daughter sat in her beautiful party dress at her own birthday celebration, tears shining on her cheeks. And Kelly had no idea it had happened.

"That's why I was asking her about the party."

"Why wouldn't Gramps tell us?"

"It's bad enough someone needed to."

"I'm sorry. You didn't tell me."

Daniel's brow furrowed. "There wasn't time. There's not a lot of time to tell you most things."

A heavy silence collapsed on them as Kelly perused the photo album. In it were strange, colorless photos of people who seemed unaware of the camera's presence. Gramps's friend Garth in one of those participation fundraisers for homeless people. Gramps in his recliner, although it was no longer burgundy but a washed-out dull pink. She turned another page and stared at the stark reality of her marriage: her and Daniel sitting on their couch unhappy at what should have been a celebration. And something was under her hand.

Was that . . . The packaging was unmistakable. She carried it around with her every day. Why would she be holding a bottle of Mendacium at Milly's party? She scanned her memory. Maybe she was talking to someone about work? That wouldn't be right. She made sure she left work at work, even more so during a family event.

Daniel inclined his head and waited for her to speak. Now she needed an answer—one she didn't have.

"What do you see in that photo?" Daniel finally asked.

So he had seen it. Kelly frowned.

Daniel reached into the briefcase and withdrew something Kelly had seen for years but never held. Gramps's camera. Daniel held it out to her as his voice rose with excitement. "He let no one touch his camera when he was alive, but he wanted me to have it. Not Mom. Me. I took it to work to show Peter, and he pointed out that all the photos have been taken. Do you know what that means?"

The weight settled onto Kelly's palm. Her fingers brushed an inscription on the bottom of the camera: *No matter what you think you might see, the camera never lies.* She peered at the tiny red *F* behind a miniature plastic window. "Gramps's last photos."

"That's right. The last photos he ever took. He's gone, but there's one last thing he wants me to do." Daniel reached for the camera. "So now I need to find somewhere to get his film processed. I don't even know where Gramps went for that. I might get Monique to find a place tomorrow."

Kelly's breath crawled out from between her teeth at the mere mention of Daniel's perky young receptionist.

Daniel threw his hands into the air. "Seriously, Kelly, every time I mention the people at work—"

Another flash of gold caught in the downlights. Kelly nodded at one cuff. "Are they a gift for Gramps's passing? From her?"

The elephant in the room. One of many. Conversations between them were becoming like a perilous night drive through a safari park. A delicate journey to avoid spooking the great beasts and being trampled. Kelly could almost feel Daniel's cogs whirring. His silence was loud. "I see."

Daniel reddened, and Kelly prepared herself for another round of a never-ending argument. Her eyes drifted up the stairs to the closed door to Milly's room. She didn't need to hear this again. Not today.

She saw that tears had welled in Daniel's eyes. "It's been a trying day, so let's not fight."

He clicked his fingers. "Also, with our

thousandth client case coming to the practice since Howard left us, we're holding a work dinner to celebrate. What do you think about hosting it here? You could cater . . ."

Another flash of gold in the downlight. Kelly placed an over-rinsed plate into the dishwasher. "That's fine. I've got a few ideas I'd like to try. So is everyone coming?"

"Of course everyone's coming. Apart from a celebration for Crossroads Counseling, Anna suggested I should focus on something fun after losing Gramps."

And there was the other name. His work-wife.

Five

Daniel strolled away from Crossroads Counseling, his final favor for Gramps bouncing along in his shirt pocket. A last chance to impress his hero.

Monique had shaken her head at Daniel's disbelief. Google was clear—only one place in the city would process his film: Simon's Film Lab. And it was just around the corner from work. Who didn't believe Google?

Daniel didn't. Who opened a new shop for something nobody needed anymore?

Hands thrust in his pockets, Daniel strolled along with a whistle on his lips and a spring of anticipation in his step. He would have the privilege of seeing these unique memories first, fresh out of the camera and even before Gramps. He hoped the quality of the photos would be better than the ones in his album.

Daniel's mission helped wash away the residue from Kelly's continued distrust. He'd all but given up convincing her that, despite all her suspicions, he'd never once violated his marriage vows. And there had been opportunities. Plenty of opportunities.

Daniel turned the corner onto Northbound

Avenue, a boulevard of leafy green that hit the middle ground of suburbia—upmarket enough to appeal to those from the higher-income brackets but welcoming enough to those who would settle for a rung on the bottom of the ladder—battling house payments and bills as much as each other.

The group of three shops was the barometer of a sputtering economy. In front of the shop on the left swung the familiar red-and-yellow paper lanterns of Ming's Court Chinese Restaurant. Daniel often bought Mr. Ming's steamed dim sims to support him before he succumbed to the economic sledgehammer of franchised food.

The shop on the right was one Daniel had neither the need nor desire to frequent. Handwritten posters filled the window: "Thursday is half-price dryer day!!" "Your dirty laundry is our forte!!" A hand-painted cardboard sign: "Coming clean! Laundromat now open!!!" What was it with exclamation points and small businesses? Beyond the paper-plastered glass, a floor-to-ceiling bank of silver washing machines ran the depth of the shop like a computer room from the 1970s.

The shop in the middle had changed. Darkness was replaced with light. The landlord's pleas for a tenant had been answered, the For Lease sign that had hung in the door for months missing. A glossy cursive on the sign above the freshly painted doorway announced Simon's Film Lab, and through the sparkling window he could see a shop dazzling in pristine white, dotted with color from framed photographs and a whole wall of cameras and lenses.

Google was right.

A tiny bell jingled as Daniel pushed open the door, and a waft of acrid chemicals stung his nose. To his left, a wall covered in photos of varying sizes, wooden, painted, and metal frames filled with people. To his right, shelves spanning the length of the wall, holding cameras of every description—large and small, old and new, black and chunky, even wooden and boxy. An exhibition on the history of photography. Each carried a tiny white price tag tied on thin cotton, fluttering as the air conditioner shunted the chemicals around the room. On higher shelves between cleaning cloths and camera bags, camera lenses stood short and tall like a Manhattan skyline. On the floor sat a row of cardboard boxes filled to the brim with tiny film canisters.

Ahead of him was a white counter, clicking and whirring coming from behind it, a small sign standing proudly on it. "Clarity like you've never experienced before!!"

From behind the counter a man rose and stood tall before rising on the balls of his feet. His face said he was midthirties, but his slicked-back silver hair hinted at an age some decades older.

He offered a broad smile to Daniel, presided over by a shining glint in his eye. He was wrapped in a white laboratory coat with a tight knot of light blue under his chin and a splash of color on his chest—a red-and-yellow name badge reading "Welcome! My name is Simon!!"

What was it with small businesses and exclamation points?

"Welcome to Simon's Film Lab! How may I help you today?"

Daniel pulled the roll of film from his shirt pocket. "I'd like to get these photos printed, please." He handed over Gramps's last memories with gravitas.

Simon inspected the canister with a quiet awe. "This is from an old camera, back from a time of proper photography." A warm voice, a slow nod, and a solemn smile. "Proper photography that meant something."

Daniel smiled at this eccentric young but old man. It was always nice to see someone who loved their work. It made a nice contrast to the stream of disaffection that sat in his office and declared this Saturday's lottery win would forever cast off the drudgery of Monday to Friday.

"My grandfather left me his camera."

The glint in Simon's eye beamed like a lighthouse beacon. "What sort of camera did he gift to you?"

Daniel should have brought it with him. "It was an old Olympus camera. HS-10, I think it said on the front."

Simon's voice dropped to an expectant whisper. "Were there any more words?"

One other drifted across Daniel's memory. "Infinity?"

The smile on Simon's face shifted into high beam as he clicked his fingers in recognition. "I know you!"

That was the downside of having your face on TV. "Yes, I'm that marriage counselor with the *No Secrets* book."

"It's wonderful to be talking with you." With a bright smile, Simon reached under the counter and produced a white plastic clipboard. He spoke to himself as he scribbled away on the form. "I don't need to ask your name, do I? Camera model is an Olympus HS-10"—he flashed a grin— "Infinity. How many copies would you like?"

That was a question Daniel hadn't even considered. You didn't in a digital age. "One, I guess. If they're any good I can always get more copies later, can't I?"

A sudden seriousness clouded Simon's face as he tapped his pen on the standee. "The HS-10 Infinity gives you great clarity." He handed over the clipboard, and Daniel scrawled his signature across the form.

Simon perused his signature with something

approaching awe. "That will be thirty-three dollars, payable now."

Daniel's eyes widened. "Thirty-three dollars?"

Simon smiled and rose again on the balls of his feet. "That's right."

"That seems steep."

Simon kept smiling.

Daniel reached for his wallet. "Well, these *are* the last photographs Gramps ever took." He would get Monique to ask Google for a second opinion.

Simon took great care to tear off the bottom part of the form and handed it over with near reverence. "This is the record of our contract."

Contract? Daniel accepted the slip, now wary of the fine line between eccentric and something to guard against.

The transaction complete, Simon burst around the counter and headed for the shelves. "You'll need more film." Giddy with excitement, he pushed a box forward with his foot. "We've got an opening special at the moment for fifty rolls of film."

Fifty? "Simon, fifty is optimistic. I'd just like one, please."

Disappointment shaded Simon's face. "But with our opening special, it would be much more cost-effective to—"

"I'm not even sure how to use the camera. One is fine."

Simon spun to face him. "The camera will be very easy to use. And once you see the clarity from an HS-10 Infinity, you'll want—"

Daniel's professional poker face slipped. "One roll."

"One?"

"Just one."

There was a slight hesitation as if Simon were weighing up the final tilt at a big sale. He smiled again and crouched over the boxes, his fingers turning film canisters. He extracted one and then placed it in Daniel's hand. "I'll tell you what, why don't I give you this roll for free? That way you can test it out. Maybe next time?"

After the frenzied enthusiasm and heavy sales pitch, this was a strange and unexpected change of gear. "Yeah, next time. That's kind of you." Monique would *have* to find another place.

A luminescent smile chased away Simon's disappointment. "Thank you so much for coming to Simon's Film Lab. I'll see you tomorrow when your photos are ready."

Daniel turned on his heel and, with the jingle of the tiny bell, left this strange shop with its photography-obsessed owner. He whistled as the single film canister nestled in his shirt pocket. He wasn't sure about this idea of clarity—the photo album didn't agree. If the camera was as good as Simon was saying, he *might* need more film, but not fifty rolls. Squeaky guitar and the first line of an early Beatles hit burst out of his pocket. "Listen . . . do you want to know a secret?"

Daniel had had the ringtone since his book launch. A love of the Beatles had been ingrained in him since a childhood spent leaning against the woven fabric and dark wood of Gramps's record player. He pulled the music from his pocket. Amanda Porter, his editor.

"Daniel! Do you have a moment?"

A numbing sense of dread engulfed him. A lurking anxiety he was fighting hard to push away.

"I do, Amanda! What's up?" He knew.

"Just following up on those emails I sent. That extension I gave you for your next book is almost up."

The numbness seeped into Daniel's bones. His sizable advance for the follow-up to *No Secrets*—their down payment on cliff-top luxury—required another book. And the numbness sank deeper with each passing day as the elusive big idea stayed in the shadows.

"You've got the advance, and we need to see something for our money."

Daniel tried to keep it light. "Yes, all still percolating."

Amanda laughed. Was it forced? "We're beyond percolating. You've already produced one bestseller, and I've already given you leeway

49

in good faith based on your success. You're now months overdue."

With a stumbled apology, Daniel hung up and shoved the phone deep into his pocket. His whistle didn't come back. Instead the icy hand of doubt clamped itself on his shoulder. Amanda was right; it should be easy for an author who'd already written one bestselling book to write another one.

But he had nothing to follow it up.

Nothing at all.

Six

The lights dimmed, and smoke snaked its way from under the heavy black curtains that lined the back of the stage. The crowd that filled the theater around Kelly dipped to a hush, and dueling colored spotlights knifed through the fog as a pulsating dance beat floated across the excited throng.

Kelly turned to Jasmine, her best friend and only friend at Rubicon Pharma. "Do we have to do this every time there's an announcement?"

"Come on, it's all part of the show. It's exciting! You loved it when you first started here." Jasmine leaned toward the stage, her eyes glued to the performance.

A middle-aged man, suit jacketed over a black T-shirt and jeans, bounced across the stage, pumping the air with his fists. The crowd of two hundred rose as one with a giant cheer for their leader. Kelly joined them on reluctant feet.

"Welcome! Welcome!" CEO Tarquin Gascon seemed to be relishing inciting the crowd to praise. Their cheers ebbed and flowed, played like the orchestra they were.

Jasmine whooped and hollered as Kelly put enough energy into her applause to be unnoticed.

"Who is the number one pharmaceutical brand in the world?" Gascon threw a hand behind his ear theatrically so his team's volume could hit 110 percent, the only number acceptable in the corridors of Rubicon Pharma.

"We are!" the crowd roared as Kelly grimaced, embarrassed at the memory of her own first days at the company when she had bought into this cult of personality.

"Friends, friends, take a seat." The crowd hushed as they settled back into their seats and Gascon steepled his fingers in front of him, strolling across the stage until he had absolute quiet.

"Two team updates for you today." He faced the throng. "First, I would like to present to you our new staff. They'll be joining our family here at Rubicon, and nothing is more important to me than team."

The commandments about teamwork hung in Kelly's cubicle, in the lunchroom, in the restrooms, and in the elevator.

Gascon ushered a lineup of what looked to be supermodels onto the stage. Young men with chiseled jaws and hair that cost a fortune to look like it cost nothing. Young women with pristine white blouses and skirts that could have passed as large belts.

Kelly pointed at the young blond woman on the end of the lineup and elbowed Jasmine. "The one on the left looks like Daniel's receptionist." Tall, thin, and fifteen years away from the battle Kelly was fighting with gravity.

"Wow, no wonder you're worried."

Gascon wandered along the line like a judge inspecting pageant contestants. "I want to introduce you to the bright young go-getters who are our executives of tomorrow. If you see them around the building, welcome them to the Rubicon family. But keep an eye on your rearview mirror, because they'll be coming up behind you."

Hollow laughter tinged with bitter nervousness rippled across the theater.

Kelly fixed her stare on the blonde at the end of the row. *So I'm being replaced by a younger model at work too.*

Gascon extracted more applause before dismissing his protégés from the spotlight, and then he clapped the crowd back into silence.

"One last thing . . . You may have read some nasty rumors about our wonder drug Mendacium and the *remote* possibility it has some *very* minor side effects."

The hush in the lecture theater was absolute as the crowd leaned forward, including Kelly. She had read about the rumors—everyone had—and if the media's accusations were even half right, the side effects were more than minor. Five-year-olds shouldn't get blinding migraines that baffle doctors.

Gascon stood center stage, waist-deep in smoke, hands open in front of him, staring into the air as if seeking divine guidance. "You have nothing to worry about."

The first smatterings of claps popped on the far side of the auditorium, and then the chattering grew as the applause built into a cacophony of cheering. A whistle from behind Kelly pierced her eardrums.

Gascon shouted over the noise as he punched the air. "Let's push on through adversity. These are just vicious attempts by our very jealous competition to bring us down!"

The crowd combusted into delirium as they leaped to their feet, and the roar ratcheted higher. Kelly turned to Jasmine to seek assurance she hadn't misheard. Gascon hadn't addressed the rumors at all.

From farther down the row, a small man with red, slicked-down hair and a permanent sneer leaned forward, his eyes drilling into her. Arnold Kolinsky, her supervisor. Kelly pumped a little more enthusiasm into her applause.

Just another few months.

Kelly and Jasmine sipped coffee in the conversational space on Level Thirteen of the palatial Rubicon Pharma building. Twenty years ago this space would have been called an alcove, but the addition of funky furniture, exposed steel beams, and spotlights introduced the concept of conversation. A defense mechanism within Kelly reminded her to lower her voice, funky furniture or not. "Was that enough of a reassurance for you?"

Jasmine looked through the steam rising from her recycled hemp cup. "If it comes from the CEO, it is. It must not be enough for you."

Colleagues wandered past as Kelly leaned forward in a conspiratorial whisper. "I think I've just had enough. It's impossible to operate at one hundred percent all the time."

Jasmine's eyes scanned the atrium as a low rumble of excitement drifted across to them. "You mean 110 percent. Do you think you're just flat after losing Gramps?"

"Maybe, but I can't shake the feeling I've had enough of being here. I was doing this only until Daniel's next book comes out. Then we'd have a bit of financial room for me to start my catering business. I can't do all that with a massive mortgage and expect to sleep at night."

"But you're so good at this job, and you're such a people person."

"It's not where my heart is. And now Milly needs me. I'm not providing what Daniel needs either. I'm sick of always feeling like I should be somewhere else."

Jasmine looked over Kelly's shoulder and talked into the cup she raised to her lips. "Keep your voice down. Tarquin is on the floor."

Kelly turned to see the CEO, hands in jeans pockets, strolling between tables.

"Jasmine, I can't keep this up."

"Fine. Then quit."

"We'd lose the house. I think I'd die if I lost that kitchen. That would be the end of my catering dream."

"Lose the house? Isn't your husband a rich and famous author?"

Kelly let out a long breath. "Bestseller might mean famous, but it doesn't automatically mean rich. We couldn't afford to buy our dream home without the advance for his second book."

"So what's the holdup?"

Staff chattered under plastic palm trees twenty feet from them. "I don't know. He should have written it by now, but every extra day is another day I have to be pushing drugs, however good they are. It's great we help so many families, but what about these side effects?"

Jasmine tapped her cup on the arm of her chair. "It's just shades of gray, isn't it? You put your product out there, and then people make their own decisions."

Kelly shrugged. "Their decisions are based on my information."

"Maybe you're just frustrated at how things are between you and Daniel. Things still bad at home?"

Kelly heaved a sigh. "Yes. And Milly's been

getting quieter for months. She won't talk to me, and Daniel keeps trying to fix her, so she won't talk to him either."

The pack of excited staff crept closer to them. "She sounds like a lot of other kids."

"But I'm Mom to only this one." Kelly gave a heavy sigh. "Daniel's just *on* all the time. I wish he'd stop trying to *fix* us and just *be* us."

"Seems weird that a marriage counselor would have a bad marriage . . . unless . . ."

"Unless what?"

"Well, if his receptionist looks like that new blonde . . ."

Kelly's eyes grazed across the atrium. She hoped no one had overheard the state of her marriage being broadcast at work.

"And what do you call his business partner again? The 'work-wife'?"

Kelly didn't know whether to rage or cry. She couldn't do either here.

"Have you suggested seeing a professional? Surely the hotshot marriage counselor believes in counseling?"

"I suggested it, and he refused." A reflex kicked in, a defense of her husband. "Daniel's a fixer—most guys are, I get that—but he's so good with the tools he uses to fix everyone else that he can't put them down when it's our problem."

Jasmine raised one eyebrow. "Really, Kel?

Honestly, to me it looks like you've got two options: confront him about it or—"

"I *have* tried confronting him, but he keeps telling me he's done nothing wrong. I don't know why I don't believe him."

"It's because your intuition isn't buying it."

Maybe Jasmine was right. Daniel *was* too defensive about the women at work. She realized she'd cut short Jasmine's answer. "What else were you going to say?"

"What do you mean?"

"You said *or*. Or what?"

"Or you could give him a wake-up call by threatening to leave."

Kelly went cold. The thought that had toyed with her for months had just been spoken aloud. The thought that had flourished the moment she opened that bank account in a pique of frustration after Daniel had tried to fix her for what seemed like the hundredth time. And while she couldn't bring herself to transfer any money to fund her defiance, she hadn't closed the account either.

Jasmine leaned forward with a cheeky grin. "That wasn't a no."

"My marriage vows were promises I meant to keep. For better or worse. This is just the worse part. I might have packed and unpacked my suitcase in my mind a few times, but I won't follow through on it."

"How much worse do you want it to get before

you do something that makes you happy again? I'm not saying you leave—just threaten to leave. Maybe that will shock him into action."

The chatter in the atrium crept closer.

"Well, that's not being honest." The other regular unwelcome thought jumped forward. If she removed herself from the picture, that would make it easier if there *was* someone else. She had to get off the topic so she could survive the rest of the day.

"So what do you think about these rumors about Mendacium and—" Jasmine stared openmouthed over Kelly's shoulder.

Kelly swung around and stared into a wall of black. Her eyes scanned up the T-shirt with a rising dread until she looked into the charismatic face of Tarquin Gascon. His jaw rippled, the twinkle in his eyes glittering like minerals in a bed of stone. "An interesting question"—he flicked a glance to her name tag—"Kelly. I'd also like to know. What do *you* think about them?"

Seven

The tiny numbers on the spreadsheet blurred as Daniel's eyelids drooped. He alt-tabbed back to the Microsoft Word window that had lurked in the background—blank—all day. The cursor blinked, a slow-ticking clock for Daniel's frustration.

He sucked in a deep breath and forced confidence into uncertain fingers as they hovered over the keys. "Chapter 1." They stopped, uninspired.

He forced his fingers into action. "Talking with Your Partner."

The cursor blinked on, and his mind remained as blank as the screen. He punched at the delete key, and it swallowed up more minutes of fruitless thinking.

"Your Successful Marriage." His impatient index finger quivered, awaiting instructions. Inspiration. Anything.

"Since *No Secrets* hit the shelves, I have spoken with thousands of people about the benefits of being honest . . ." His fingers slowed. He was boring even himself.

With a sweep of his mouse, he deleted yet another opening paragraph that didn't deserve its place on the page. The cursor blinked on.

Daniel yawned as he stretched, looking at the pile of books stacked on his office desk. The second book—the one his contract demanded— had started as an impossibility and had since become even harder. He stared out the window at his car in the darkened, almost-empty parking lot.

Maybe Anna's experience could provide inspiration. At least she would know where to start.

A light tap sounded from his doorway. Daniel spun to see his receptionist leaning against the door, a half smile dangling from those ruby-red lips.

"Monique, shouldn't you have gone home by now?"

"You said you were working late. Do you need anything from me?"

A blaring alarm went off in Daniel's head. The scenario he'd warned hundreds of couples about for years unfolded in front of him.

"No, but thanks for offering."

"I'm more than happy to stay if you need me. You spend so much time helping other people, I thought *you'd* appreciate help for a change."

"No, that's fine—"

She rushed to sit on the edge of his sofa, crossing long legs just feet from him. "Could I ask a question? For a friend?"

Daniel smirked. That old chestnut. He'd

counseled more "friends" in his office than actual clients.

"Sure! For a 'friend.' "

Monique seemed to measure her words as she stared at the carpet. "This friend of mine is struggling to keep her head above water in life and feels like she needs to hide who she is." She looked up under slowly batting lashes.

Maybe he could help. Daniel laced his fingers behind his head. "I'd suggest your friend talk to someone. There's no point keeping secrets if they aren't helpful in the long run."

"She just wants to be noticed by the right people. The right person." Her eyes drifted to the flash of gold on his cuff, and the corners of her mouth tugged into a grin.

The alarm in Daniel's head blared again, cutting across his growing comfort in the conversation. He hit the metaphorical snooze button. This was manageable.

"I suggest your friend is not aware of how people see her."

Monique's cheeks flushed as she smoothed her skirt. The siren blared.

"Do you think so? She's at a crossroads in life, if you'll pardon the pun." A light laugh fluttered from her lips, and she recrossed her long legs.

Daniel's smile eased across his face before his conscience elbowed him to wake up. He had to stop. He was due home. He was due anywhere except here.

"What do you suggest my friend do to get the attention of the right man?"

The internal struggle in Daniel roared to life. The flirting was enticing—enchanting even—but he couldn't act on it. He was married, and Monique was an employee. "Well, for your friend—and let's be clear here that my advice is for 'your friend'—I suggest she ensure other people don't form the basis of her self-esteem."

Monique nodded, her lips parting. "But how can she find happiness?"

This conversation had to become a formal counseling session, and with Anna, but the part of him that was enjoying the flirtation had one final thing to give. "I would say what I say to most people. You have to be true to yourself."

He cringed. Those words sounded worse out loud than in his head. "What I meant to say is that if it's appropriate, then you should be true—"

Monique beamed as her cheeks flushed. "You don't have to tell me twice!"

Daniel had lit a touch paper, and he needed to douse it. Quickly. "Is this about a friend, or should I do something to help you out as a boss? My hope here at Crossroads is that we can all be honest with each other, no secrets and all that. If you need to speak to someone, I would suggest Anna—"

Monique smoothed her skirt again and gestured to the family photo on his desk. "You look happy there. How long ago was that?"

The photo of a loving husband and father was more dated with each passing day.

And Monique wasn't leaving.

With an extravagant stretch, Daniel stood. "I appreciate your offer of help, but I need to finish some important things. Enjoy your evening."

She rose in a mirror to his actions, and they stood face-to-face, inches apart. Monique's smile smoldered on her lips as time slowed to a drip. The silence moved from discomfort to promise . . . and back again.

Squeaky guitar and a few nasal lines of an early Beatles hit burst out of his pocket. "Listen . . . do you want to know a secret?"

Daniel scrambled for his phone. Kelly. Relief morphed into dread. The escape route from this conversation would come with a price.

"I have to take this. It's Kelly. Enjoy your evening."

Monique sagged into a frown and turned on her heel. Thankfully.

Daniel threw back his head and exhaled hard as he picked up the call. "Hi, Kel."

There was a moment in space, a silence and hesitation. And then a flat voice. "Are you on your way home yet? I need to talk to you about work today."

Daniel stared at the blinking cursor on his screen. "I'm about to leave. Just finishing up a few things."

Another moment of silence, pregnant with an unasked question. "Are there a few of you working late on something?" A pointed reference veiled under a direct question.

"There's no need to be like that." He heard the front door to the practice close after Monique. "I'm the only one here, just getting through some financial stuff and writing the new book."

Another moment of silence.

"Look, I'll be home soon. Would you like me to pick up some noodles from around the corner?"

He heard her sigh down the phone line. "We've already eaten."

"I'm just leaving now. I'll be home in about thirty minutes."

"Dinner is in the microwave." She cut the call.

Daniel's eyes returned to the flashing, accusing cursor that stood between him and the fulfillment of his book contract. He had no idea where the words would come from. He lowered the lid on his laptop as he checked off the battles he was fighting with a wife who didn't believe he was doing nothing wrong and a receptionist who couldn't believe he wouldn't.

Eight

Kelly stomped out of the clinic into spitting rain and ran for the parking lot, powered by a cocktail of emotions: simmering anger and numbing fear. It wasn't just the doctors complaining about the quality of their free lunch. It was more than the barbs about golf clubs needing an upgrade.

She flung her bag of Mendacium samples into the back seat and slammed the door shut as a curtain of rain fluttered across her windshield.

She was the second Rubicon Pharma rep who'd visited that day. And based on the drooling description of the young intern who asked Kelly if she could get hold of a phone number, she knew who'd been there.

The blonde from the stage. The new staff weren't in her rearview mirror; they were cutting her off in traffic and threatening to steal her car.

Kelly stared through the rain as her heart reached for what it knew she needed—to talk to Daniel. But her head reminded her how difficult that would be after he'd leaned against the bathroom door that morning and asked in a not-so-subtle way about the need for so much makeup at work. And at the mention of competing with the supermodels Gascon had just hired, he'd just narrowed his eyes and studied her. She'd bailed out of the conversation before it became another one of *those* discussions.

Kelly tapped her forehead on the steering wheel. She knew who she had to talk to and punched in the number.

"Arnold Kolinsky."

Kelly's breath threatened to derail her. *Keep it professional.*

"It's Kelly. Another sales rep went to see one of my clinics today."

A stream of obscenities flowed into her car, surfing on a rising tide of her supervisor's trademark bitterness. "I bet it's Taraxa or Adversarius. What you need to do is go back there—"

"It was another rep from Rubicon."

"Right." Then silence.

Right?

"Was that all, Kelly?"

Is that all? She was being cut out of a job by her own company.

"This is a competitive business, so you need to compete." Arnold's oily breath closed off his sentence.

"But they're *my* clients. What about in yesterday's team meeting when Mr. Gascon said—"

Kelly could feel the icicles forming on the other end of this conversation.

"Mr. Gascon came to see me yesterday. In person." The hard edge in his voice suggested this was nothing to celebrate. "He told me you challenged him over these unfounded rumors concerning Mendacium."

Kelly shaped her mouth to respond, but nothing came out.

Arnold jumped into the space she'd left. "All you did yesterday was make a fool out of our entire team, but most importantly, you made a fool out of me. When you're on company time, you put the team first. You sell the product and its wonders in treating screen addiction in children. You have your sales scripts, and you have the mentoring program if you need help reading them. You need to give 110 percent to survive in this business."

Kelly couldn't help herself. "Arnold, I think integrity stands out."

A bitter laugh. "I know people with integrity. They're the ones who take my coffee order in the morning."

Tears welled and watered blooming resentment. Thank goodness this wasn't a video call.

"Understood, Kelly?"

"Understood."

Kelly hated just one thing more than not being heard, and that was being lectured. She grasped at the right way to end this call. To save face. But Arnold saved her the trouble.

Kelly rested her forehead on the steering wheel, this time unable to hold back a tsunami of tears. The job that was supposed to be temporary was day by day becoming more permanent—and was eating her alive.

The knife came down hard on the board as Kelly chopped at onions that brought even more tears. She mulled over the best way to start the conversation with Daniel when he got home. Long ago they could have talked for hours without an agenda. Now she needed to script how to even begin.

She looked up through the tears to see Daniel looking at her, his head cocked, his brow unknotted. "What's the matter?"

Kelly put down the knife and dissolved. Daniel leaped forward and wrapped her in his arms.

After a few moments, Kelly stepped back and wiped her eyes. "I'm sorry."

"What for? Obviously something's wrong."

The mess of her day flooded out of her. "I'm being cut out of my job by my own company, and I don't think I can take any more." The sobs racked her. "And Milly needs me . . . and I can't keep lying like that . . . and with Gramps going . . ." Her hurricane of emotions dragged in every other sadness of life into her storm of tears.

"Let's talk about one thing at a time. What do you mean being cut out by your own company?"

Kelly stepped back from the counter. "A new bunch of reps who look like they've stepped off the catwalk are now my competition. One young woman visited my clients today and tried to sweep them out from underneath me." Her voice hardened as her anger flickered back to life.

"Can you complain about it? Isn't there some kind of process for making sure your company doesn't do that?"

Kelly laughed through the stinging tears. "I did complain. All Arnold did was tell me to compete harder."

"You said you can't keep lying like that. What did you mean?"

"There are rumors that Mendacium has serious side effects—giving young children untreatable splitting migraines, among other things. Gascon said today he'd address them, but he didn't, and I have to tell doctors that our product is fine."

Milly walked into the kitchen with her phone raised in front of her face and a slight smile.

Kelly glanced back at Daniel in time to see his brow furrow. *Please, Daniel, not now.*

"Can you confront them at work and ask for some evidence so you can be honest with your clients?"

Kelly felt the disconnection with a jolt. *Just listen to me.* "If I do that I'll lose my job . . . which won't be a bad thing, necessarily."

Kelly felt Daniel tense. Their usual sticking point, the barnacled reef on which conversations foundered. Milly thumbed in her earbuds and disappeared up the stairs.

"Can you hang on for another month or two?"

Kelly stood back from Daniel and wiped her eyes. "Why is it taking so long?"

Daniel snorted. "It just is."

Kelly closed her eyes. "I'm not sure how much longer I can hang on. And Milly needs me now." She opened her eyes to Daniel's pursed lips. Those knitted brows.

"But if you quit now, we could lose the house and everything we've been working toward. I'm trying as hard as I can."

In that moment, Kelly saw the husband she once knew, not one head down and charging ahead but one without all the answers. "It's nice to talk again. We used to talk about everything. What happened to those days?"

"It happens to a lot of couples when they get busy or hit this stage in life. It's normal."

"Is that what you say to the couples you work with? Things are normal?"

The question was innocent enough as it left Kelly's lips, but it seemed to reach Daniel's ears with a pointed intent. He dropped his eyes and

71

strode toward his study, head down, back to his regular distance.

Kelly grabbed the knife. The tears came back as she chopped again at the already chopped onions. She would love to go back to those happier days when the world was in front of them and they were tackling it together rather than it squeezing in on them and pushing them apart. Jasmine's comment burrowed in deeper under her skin as thoughts she never imagined possible danced around her. Keeping open an empty account at a strange bank. Leaving the man she'd promised to love forever. Returning to their early days would be impossible, but she could force better days ahead.

What would *life be like if I left?* A daydream scrolled across her mind, one in which she packed her suitcase and threw it in the back of the car, and then drove away from all this baggage.

Nine

The tiny bell jingled, and the waft of chemicals again pinched Daniel's nose. The smell of something developing.

On a small sign sitting on the unattended counter, a smiling cartoon camera checked its oversized wristwatch: "Back in a minute!" Another relic from another time.

At the back of the lab, a white-and-blue behemoth of right angles and metal took up half the floor space with a gentle hum and occasional clicks. Another relic, from a time when the larger the technology, the more its sophistication.

Daniel made his way to the shelves, drawn in by a wooden box, concertinaed leather separating rich mahogany. The camera sat in the shelf's center, its thick lens beaming like a cyclops. A burnished gold plaque on the front carried the proud name of its maker: Cameo 1915. This camera was more than a hundred years old but somehow also new. A tiny white square hung from a cotton thread tied to a wooden arm. Daniel gave a low whistle at the handwritten price—$10,000 or W.I.N. These old cameras were valuable. And those initials must represent a photographic term.

A dusty, scratched, black-and-beige box sat next to the Cameo, on top a thick, dirty-white serrated plastic knob and a small cylindrical trigger also in plastic. On the camera's face was a recessed lens beneath a scratched red label: Kodak. This camera had lived a life.

Daniel fingered the tiny white square that hung from it: $95 or W.I.N. It must not work. This would interest only someone who wanted to relive long-forgotten childhood memories.

Farther along the shelf the cameras evolved with the decades. Shining silver replaced dark wood. The black was a constant but moved from leather to plastic. At the end of the shelf sat a stout, proud camera with a large hooded bulb hovering over it like a gargoyle on a stone crypt. A technological marvel of its day, but its thick buttons and cogs now out of place in a world of screens. Its tiny white paper square announced $500 or W.I.N.

Daniel picked it up and squinted through the viewfinder. The cameras on the shelves sprang to life, the leather now new, the wood buffed, the silver polished. Razor-sharp edges and fine detail. Simon wasn't kidding; the clarity was incredible.

Daniel swung around to see what the camera would make of the frames on the opposite wall. Slick, parallel lines of silver hair filled his vision, and Daniel jumped a mile.

"There's just something about the clarity old cameras provide, isn't there?"

Daniel fumbled to put the camera back on the shelf. "You scared the life out of me!"

"I hope not. Life is all we have. That, and truth."

Simon reached for the wooden camera with the concertina nose, his voice a reverent whisper. "This is the best photography, capturing moments of reality. It's not like today's technology where software and filters create a world we'd like to believe is real and photographs are deleted because they're not perfect."

Daniel forced the cadence from his voice. His professional voice. "You love cameras, don't you?"

Simon smiled, his eyes drifting beyond Daniel to the shelves. "I love the truth my cameras show. We can't trust our memories. They gloss over details, change words to ones we wish we'd used, and bury the secrets we try to hide. Photos give us clear memories and show us what really happened. The camera never lies, you know."

Daniel's breath deserted him. The phrase from the bottom of Gramps's camera.

"The camera reveals how our lives truly are. We can't trick it, even if sometimes we think we can trick ourselves and everyone around us."

Daniel chuckled. "You should be a counselor."

"Why is that?"

"You seem to have great clarity, to use your word. That's what you need when you're dealing with people's issues."

"And your own, I suspect."

Daniel was taken aback at the sudden switch in the conversation. Simon grinned at Daniel as he placed the camera back on the shelf, and then he clicked his fingers and dropped to his haunches. "That reminds me, once you get your photos back, you'll want more film." He pulled a box from under the shelves. "Because of the great clarity of the Olympus HS-10 Infinity, you'll need a box. We've got an opening special on fifty—"

Daniel grunted to put an end to the sales pitch before it eroded even more of his morning. "You gave me one last time. I'm not sure I need another—the photos Gramps took were not very clear at all. In fact, the color was washed out."

A grin crept across Simon's face and froze into place. "I know. It's wonderful, isn't it?"

Wonderful? "All I want is Gramps's last photos."

Simon swept an arm toward the frames on the far wall. "But don't you see? These photographs will provide you with great insight and reveal so much about life."

Daniel looked across the room to the faces framed in dark timber, ornate painted wood, silver, and metal. And at an empty frame closest to the counter.

"Simon, look—"

A soft buzz emanated from the blue-and-white machine. Simon jumped up and sprinted behind the counter, pulling on white gloves. He reached for a handful of photographs from the racks nestled into one side of the processing machine, smiling as he counted his way through them. He put them in an envelope and raced back to the counter, peeled a sticker from a roll under the counter, and sealed the envelope with great care. He held it out to Daniel with a solemn nod. "This is always a big moment, when people find out what their cameras have captured."

Daniel grasped the envelope, but Simon still held on to it. Daniel pulled a little harder, and Simon let go. He would ask Monique to consult Google again for another processing place. One online even.

Simon rose again on the balls of his feet. "I trust those photographs show you what you need to see. And you can have that roll of film."

Daniel quick-stepped out of this strange conversation, and the tiny bell jingled at his escape.

The sticker on the envelope—a replica of an old-fashioned wax seal—proclaimed that Simon's Film Lab provided "greater clarity than you've ever had for those moments in life that matter the most." The weight of the moment settled onto Daniel. He peeled away the sticker and steeled himself for the emotion he knew would come. In his hand, he held the last images Gramps cared enough about to capture before he passed away.

The first photo showed Anna Potts in deep conversation with a couple as they sat in her office.

What?

Daniel flicked through the envelope. The staff of Crossroads Counseling appeared in every photo. These weren't Gramps's last memories. Someone in the practice had used his camera. Annoyance bit deep into him. It had to be Peter, the photography buff, but encroaching on personal space like that was out of character for him.

So who took the photos?

"Excuse me!" A woman with a laundry basket full of clothes pushed past him and into the laundromat.

Daniel sputtered an apology, still reeling from the intrusion into his privacy. He would raise it at their staff meeting tomorrow.

He flicked through the photographs again. Anna counseled a couple. Cameron, his business manager, stared out his office window as if dreaming of somewhere else. Jade, his practice manager, had her cell phone pressed into a tearstained cheek. Ordinary photos of ordinary people doing ordinary things. And echoes of the photos from Gramps's album—his staff didn't even know their photo was being taken.

In the next photo Anna stood in his office doorway, staring beyond the camera, her head tilted, her cheeks flushed under a faraway stare. He'd never seen her like that, and why would he?

Monique winked at the camera and blew a kiss to whoever was holding it. He reached for his cuffs. So it wasn't her.

Two faces weren't represented: his and Peter's. Friend and colleague aside, a line had been crossed.

In another photo, papers were strewn across a desk, a mix of bills and bank statements. Maybe this photo belonged to someone else and Simon had mixed up two orders when pulling them from the film processor.

In the final photo, a book sat on his office chair. A familiar book. The sharp contrast of two words in chunky black writing on a stark white cover. Two words burned into his memory.

No Secrets.

But something was missing—something he'd seen thousands of times, something that had brought mixed emotions when he saw it for the first time. Pride. Nerves.

His name.

Below the title was white space where his name usually sat. His name had been erased.

Daniel's mouth went dry as a memory knocked at a long-shut-off door in his mind.

He needed to know two things.

Who took this photo?

And why?

Ten

Han Solo stood tall on the desk in front of Kelly as Dr. Anthony Scott tweaked Chewbacca and Yoda in the line of Star Wars figurines. "This is the downside of keeping children distracted during a diagnosis."

The soft smiles of animal puppets filled the shelves behind the doctor, and a haphazard, jagged Lego castle teetered on a pint-size table to her left.

Kelly looked back to the doctor and into his searching gaze. "Kelly, I need to ask you about Mendacium."

Another news alert about the side effects of Rubicon Pharma's wonder drug had woken Kelly. The company was shutting down the media's questions instead of answering them.

"It's a wonderful drug that's already helped dozens of the children I see when it comes to screen addiction—and I'm grateful for what it delivers. I'm booked up for months with parents wanting to see me for a prescription, so it's good for the practice. But when I see stories about untreatable migraines in small children, I need to ask questions."

Kelly flicked a glance at the puppets on the

shelf and felt a kinship. "I've seen those rumors as well, but I've spoken directly with our CEO, and he advises me there is nothing to worry about."

Kelly weighed that statement and found no lies.

The doctor steepled his fingers in front of his face and drilled her with sparkling blue eyes. "So you can give me a guarantee that Mendacium is safe to prescribe?"

Kelly balanced on the high wire of the company line and delicately toed it. "What I can tell you, Anthony, is that the information I've been given from my company is that there's nothing to worry about." Each word in that sentence passed inspection.

Anthony's gaze was unrelenting. "I hope you're right, because I have two patients after lunch who are glued to their devices. Really young kids too. This would be the obvious treatment, but if there are risks, I won't hesitate to drop Mendacium, no matter how much of a wonder drug it is."

Kelly was sure her pulse throbbed an inch out of her temples. "I think you'll be fine." She didn't bother to evaluate that statement, taken verbatim from the morning's all-staff email. The script for the day.

Anthony's eyes flashed a softer blue. "Thanks for not overselling me or offering to distract my medical opinion with tickets to the ballet like the other reps seem to love doing. I appreciate your honesty."

Kelly smiled, although a tinge of guilt tugged at its corners.

Dr. Scott stood and extended a hand. "It's wonderful to see you, as always."

Anthony's soft palm surprised Kelly as a playfulness danced in his eyes.

"Lovely to see you, Anthony—as always."

She withdrew her hand, too slowly, hoping to finish the conversation on a good note before one too many questions was thrown out. The high wire beckoned again.

The doctor ushered her to the door. "Speaking of other reps, my practice manager has booked in an appointment late this afternoon with someone else from Rubicon. Why do I need visits from two reps?"

Kelly's head dropped before steel took over her voice. "You can cancel that appointment, Anthony. I'll take care of your needs."

"Good to know. Take care."

Kelly left the doctor's office, buoyed with the win, however minor. It was good to have one.

The minimal wording from the CEO's email elbowed its way into her thinking. And the ember of the lie she'd just given Anthony Scott, savior of children with a damaging obsession with a tiny screen, burned slow in her heart.

Eleven

Daniel forced his fingers onto the keys of his laptop. "Chapter 1." His fingers stopped, directionless. The cursor blinked on, and those two words stood alone on the screen.

He stared at the ceiling, exhaling hard. He knew coming up with an idea for the next book would be difficult, but this difficult?

"You wanted to see me, Daniel?" Jade stood in his doorway, looking nervous, fumbling fingers searching for something to hold.

"I did. Come in." Daniel reached for a box of tissues as she sat down on his sofa, her gaze anywhere but in his direction.

Daniel leaned in and whispered, "Is everything okay?"

Jade's emotions burst from her as she snatched for the tissues. "It's my dad. Secondary cancer." She dabbed at the tears in her eyes. "How did you know?"

Daniel handed over the box. How could he answer that question? "I just wanted to check in with you to make sure you're okay." Daniel examined his statement for a lie and found none.

Jade sucked in racking sobs. "But I just

found out about it yesterday. I've tried to be professional at work and not bring my stuff into the office . . ."

"But I would hope you could talk about things going on in your life."

Jade looked up at him through the tears. "But your timing is incredible. It's almost as if you knew . . . But how could you know?"

Daniel couldn't divulge the answer to that question. "If you want to take some personal time to handle your dad's health . . ."

Jade pressed a finger to shakily smiling lips. "Thank you for understanding. You have a gift of insight into people."

The usual compliment soured. Daniel knew there was something else; there was *someone* else. Whoever took that photograph of Jade was the one with the real insight. And he was about to find out who it was.

Ten unreadable faces sat around the boardroom at Crossroads Counseling.

Daniel scanned them. Again. Two hints at personal space and nothing. His team presented a blank page.

"Just to close our meeting, Anna has come up with a brilliant idea for a major milestone here at Crossroads. Our thousandth client has come through our doors."

Monique let out a soft squeal.

"She's suggested a dinner to celebrate, so I would like you all, everyone who has contributed to the success of Crossroads, to come to our place up on Clifftop Drive. Kelly and I will be pleased to welcome you to our home."

Monique squealed again into rising chatter around the table. This time the room was easy to read.

Anna took over the conversation. "It was just a small suggestion to celebrate the wonderful work we do here, and I think we deserve to celebrate!"

Daniel studied his staff. Maybe he needed to be more direct to give the person responsible the chance to own their intrusion into his privacy. "We've done great work here with the couples and families who've come to us." He couldn't help himself. He had to know. "But I want to say, if there's anything you'd like to tell me, my door is always open."

Jade threw him a nod and a teary smile as the room quieted at Daniel's sudden, awkward prying into their personal lives. He surveyed his team, looking for something. Anything. There was no reaction, save Monique's beaming grin.

"So if there's nothing more"—Daniel again surveyed the room for a response—"let's get back to work!"

The meeting broke up with wary chatter.

Monique sidled up to Daniel, her eyes roaming his wrists.

"It's such a great achievement to think we've saved a thousand marriages." Her perfume wafted toward him and reached for his throat. "And I'd love to see your home."

Daniel stepped back to breathe professional distance into the conversation. Monique's perfume edged forward. Behind Monique's shoulder Anna's eyebrow rose.

"I'm not sure we've saved a thousand marriages, but we have at least tried. And it will be a great night of celebration for us all."

Daniel burst through the heady cloud and brushed past Monique on his way to his office. He'd lobbed indirect mentions of Gramps's camera into the meeting, but there'd been no ripples. He had given the perpetrator the chance to come clean, but now he'd have to address each employee one at a time. Starting with Peter. But now there was a fresh problem. Anna's eyebrow was on his case, and he was sure she would raise the issue of Monique again sooner rather than later.

A soft rapping came at his door. Okay, sooner.

Daniel didn't even turn around. "I know what you're going to say."

But Anna didn't respond.

"Wow, famous counselor and now mind reader?" Peter stepped into his office and perched himself on the center of Daniel's sofa.

Daniel backpedaled, searching for a one-liner that would turn an embarrassing revelation—and something a crack observer like Peter would latch onto—into a joke. "I've just done the finances, and I can't afford to double your pay so you can get what you're worth."

"You'll never be able to afford what I'm worth." Peter chuckled before drilling a look into Daniel. "I won't keep you because we've both got clients, but is everything okay? In our meeting you made two veiled references to personal space and a couple of digs about your door always being open."

The moment to address Peter presented itself. "I'm glad you've raised it. I had Gramps's camera on my desk all day yesterday, but as you pointed out, the film was already used up."

"Gramps's last photos. Have you got them back yet?" The slate of Peter's expression remained blank.

"Yes, and they were all of people at work. The entire roll of film." Daniel left the point hanging in the air.

Peter's stony gaze remained. "So who do you think it was?"

Daniel steepled his fingers under his nose, allowing space in the conversation for Peter to fill. But unlike his clients, Peter was comfortable facing a weapon he himself wielded with ease.

"My first thought was you."

Peter's reaction wasn't scrambling for an answer or fumbling for an apology. He reddened in offense.

"You know me better than that." He shifted on the sofa. "So was that what your comments were all about? You were ticked off that someone used your camera? Why didn't you just ask?"

Daniel couldn't share his answer. It was more than someone using his camera. He needed to know who would take a photo of his book and erase his name from the cover.

"And one of the photos was of my book." He again left that point hanging in the air.

Peter's brow furrowed, and he studied his boss. "Well, we're all fans of *No Secrets* around here, so it could have been any of us, I guess."

Monique's beaming smile leaned into the doorway. "Peter, your nine thirty is here."

Peter headed for the doorway but then turned. "Just be honest with me next time, okay? And if I can say this as a friend—for all of us—we have to practice what we preach." Peter nodded at the pile of books on Daniel's desk. "And what we write about in bestselling books."

Daniel stared at the pile, and the nonappearance of his second book again reared its head. That was another part of his life where the pressure was an ever-tightening ratchet.

A rapping came at his door, and a burgundy streak in defiance of gray appeared halfway up his doorway.

And this was another.

Twelve

Kelly stood in Gramps's favorite room, the afternoon sunlight warming her shoulders as it streamed through thinning, sheer white curtains. His tiny apartment felt smaller. They had removed only two boxes, but the place felt lesser for it. Only an old burgundy suede recliner pointed at a tiny television in the corner remained, the seat and armrests shiny from use. Hanging over one armrest was the sling containing his remote control and dog-eared crossword book.

One last room, and Gramps would be consigned to memory. An entire life lived, a rocky path forged, a complete journey navigated, and they were about to put the last of him into a box for disposal.

Daniel's mother walked into the room, dabbing at her eyes. All afternoon Charlotte had turned each item she touched over in her hands, the memories flooding back along with tears.

"How is work, love?" Charlotte sniffled onto another subject.

Kelly sighed. "It's tough at the moment."

"Can't you stay home with Milly?"

Kelly's preferred answer was easy. Reality was anything but. "No."

"Could you take another job closer to home?"

Kelly tried to roll the rising tension from her shoulders. "My friend got me this one, and that took a while. Anyway, I won't be there much longer, just until Daniel gets the rest of his advance."

Milly walked into the room swinging a pair of tortoiseshell reading glasses in her fingers. "What should I do with these?"

Kelly stared at the thick lenses that no longer held a twinkle behind them. Milly placed the glasses in Kelly's hand before withdrawing her phone from her pocket as she slid down the wall to the floor.

Charlotte rushed over to Milly with all the fluster of a startled hen. "Are you okay, beautiful?"

Milly looked up, her face bathed in the low light of her ever-present screen. "I know he's already gone, but it feels like we're packing him away, that's all."

Kelly couldn't have put it better herself.

Charlotte stroked Milly's hair. "How are you doing in school? I haven't seen a report card for a while."

Milly gripped the phone tighter, her thumbs now stiff hammers tapping at the screen. "Okay, I guess."

Kelly could see it wasn't. Come to think of it, she hadn't seen a report card either.

Hands on hips, Daniel stood in the doorway. "Well, this is it. Gramps didn't have much, did he?"

Charlotte's voice lowered to a whisper. "He never did."

Daniel's brow furrowed. "Gramps was a gambler, after all."

"Was he?" Charlotte sank onto the recliner, her hand covering her mouth. "So that's what he meant when he said he'd beaten something that had beaten him." She frowned as the tears came back. "How did you know? And why would he tell you but not me?"

"He didn't, but a photo in his album shows him tearing up a betting slip. I thought you must have known."

"I never saw that photo, and he never showed me his album."

"I guess he didn't want to disappoint you."

"I guess not. That was so like him." Her eyes clouded again. "It was special that he left that camera to you. May I ask what was in the letter?"

Kelly snapped a look at Daniel. "What letter?"

Daniel stared at his feet. "There was a letter with the camera."

Kelly hoped he would fill the silence with more, but Daniel moved past her and grabbed the television. Then he left the room.

Milly's voice floated up from the floor. "Why can't you and Dad just talk?"

Kelly was struggling to come to grips with that question herself. She flicked a glance at Charlotte, now a wide-eyed observer to the obvious conflict. "It's not that easy sometimes when you're a couple."

"I thought it would be easier if one of you was a marriage counselor." Milly's comment hung in the air as she stared harder into her screen.

"No, it's not easier. We're both still people. But I would prefer it if we were all just honest with each other in our family."

Milly's eyes clouded.

"Actually, Milly, I haven't seen your school report either."

Milly snapped a look at her, and then she slid back up the wall and headed for the door.

Kelly watched her leave. How bad must her report be? And what was in the letter from Gramps? Even if it was personal, why wouldn't Daniel share it with her? She shook herself out of her thoughts to see her mother-in-law studying her, eyes flicking between Milly's back and Kelly's confusion.

She rose from the recliner and put a hand on Kelly's arm. "How are you three doing?"

"We're busy, but so is everyone. Daniel's business is flying."

"I'm so proud of the success of his practice."

"Well, he's spending enough time there." An opportunity presented itself, a chance to grill

Charlotte about Daniel. "Does he ever mention work to you?"

"Sometimes he keeps me up-to-date."

Kelly tried hard to keep her voice light, almost nonchalant. "Does he mention the staff at all?"

"Sometimes, but it's more about the people he helps, isn't it?"

Not really. Kelly pushed one more time. "Do the same names come up?"

"I don't think so." She peered at Kelly. "Love, if there's anything you need to know, you just need to ask him yourself." And with that she left the room.

Kelly felt her hackles rise in response to the condescension. It wasn't that she'd been lectured about her marriage but that she *had* asked Daniel time and again. Yet he was a closed book. Or an angry open one.

Daniel reappeared in the doorway, rubbing his hands. "It's just so final. The recliner, and that's it. We're not giving this away. It's going in my study." He moved past her to pick it up.

Kelly turned to leave behind the memory of Gramps's favorite room, the job of packing him away almost complete. Why wouldn't her husband talk about the letter?

"Kelly? What's this?" Beneath the cushion he'd taken off was a photograph. Daniel picked it up and looked at it closely. "That's a bank statement, isn't it? Beyond Bank—never heard of them before."

The blood drained from Kelly's face. *She* had heard of them before.

Daniel peered at the photograph even closer. "Why would Gramps take a photo of that?"

Kelly snatched it from him. "No idea. I'll ask your mother." She had to get that photo away from Daniel in case the name on the account was hers.

Thirteen

The clouds hung over the ocean, whiter than they'd ever been. Lines of breaking waves feathered out from rocks Daniel had seen a hundred times from the cliff top, but now they thrust out of the water in a rich, lime-green coat of seaweed. The tall grass whipped at his legs, and the white-and-yellow flower heads that lined the path swept back and forth with vibrant life.

Daniel lowered Gramps's camera from his eye as the salty wind whipped his cheeks and tousled his hair. The clouds grayed over the muddy ocean. Simon might be at the annoying end of eccentric, but he was right about the camera's clarity. This was his first chance to try it out. Finally.

Behind him, Milly dragged her feet in the low-slung flowers. They'd always been close—many people said she was definitely his daughter—and what hurt him most was their growing distance. He could quote the textbook signs of teenage rebellion in his sleep, but he still wanted her to be his little princess, not the saddened version of a princess locked in a tower of her own making. He needed to fix her.

Milly caught his eye and veered off the path

toward the cliff's edge. A tingle of parental anxiety leaped up Daniel's spine.

"Dad, how long do you think it would take to reach the bottom if you jumped?"

They also shared a dark humor. "Good one, Mill." Daniel studied her for signs of honesty rather than humor. He lifted the camera to his eye again, and she appeared in his vision, one foot off the cliff.

"Milly!" Daniel all but dropped the camera as he rushed forward to grab his daughter.

She was no longer on the edge. She stood by the path, hands in pockets. "What?"

"If you think it's funny, it isn't."

"Is what funny?"

A light wind whipped between them as Milly approached him. "Can I hold Gramps's camera?"

Daniel held it out to her, and she took it, her hands dipping with the weight. She inspected its size and then ran a finger along the knobs on its top and the window on its back. "How does the film work?"

"It goes in the back, runs across the lens, is collected on the other side, winds back, and then you take the canister to a film processing place."

Milly lifted the camera to her eye and scanned the horizon. "Film processing place? Why not just download them?"

"Download them?" Daniel laughed. "No, I

have to take them to a film lab. Monique found one around the corner from work."

Milly handed the camera back to Daniel. Through its lens he focused on the distant cliffs where the path wound its way back inland. Sharp detail carved into the vertical drops, each blade of long, thin grass on the outcrops waving in the sea breeze. Trees that fought hard to poke out from the cliff drew stark white lines on the brown and ochre rock.

Daniel squeezed the trigger with a satisfying *clunk*—a mechanical one he felt in his fingers, not a sound fashioned by an audio engineer.

Milly sat on a large rock that forced the meandering path wide, her chin in her hands, her eyes down. Daniel's heart sank. The same pose as at her birthday party.

He had to know.

Daniel sat down next to her on the mammoth rock. "We didn't finish our chat about your birthday party—"

Milly's chin shot out of her hands, her eyes cloaked in suspicion. "Why do you keep asking me about that?"

"I'm just checking in. We don't get to talk like we used to, so I'm just making sure you're okay."

The cloak remained as Milly folded angry arms. "So that's why you wanted me to come with you? And why are you trying to fix me? Why don't you try to fix you and Mom?"

Daniel's mind shifted gears as Milly raised the stakes. "You know, when people change the subject after being asked an uncomfortable question—"

Milly stood in a rush. "Which is what you've just done."

She *was* like him. *So* like him.

"I'm not stupid, you know. I can see what's going on." Her eyes searched Daniel's in what he thought was desperation, hoping he would take the reins of a conversation that was racing away from her.

Daniel had to proceed with kid gloves. For the first time in a long time, Milly had opened a crack in the door she'd shut between them.

"So how is school?"

Milly crossed her arms again. "Maybe if you paid more attention to Mom, my family wouldn't feel like it was falling apart." And after lobbing that grenade at him, she stormed back along the path to home.

"Milly!"

She slowed ever so slightly before increasing her pace. She wasn't coming back, and rushing after her would only make things worse.

One positive thought broke through his growing frustration. He now knew what was bugging her. He walked a little farther along the path and again lifted the camera to his eye. Foaming white sea spray surged over the rocks below, and as the ocean retreated from its pulsing attack, the lime-green seaweed glistened in the afternoon sun. Daniel again squeezed the trigger.

Milly's words burned, even though they gave him a plan.

Work again elbowed its way into his thoughts. It was flattering to have Monique's attention, to feel the buzzing pulse of youth. But he would need to reinforce the boundaries. He was proud of his efforts to be a man of integrity. A few patients had thrown themselves at him—he was an obvious white knight to some—but he'd always stayed true to his wedding vows. At least Anna had his back.

The grass whipped at his shins as Daniel plowed along. He lifted the camera to his eye, and the flowers came alive, their yellow-and-white faces basking in the afternoon sun. Another satisfying *clunk*. An uncomfortable thought perched in his mind. If the camera was this good, why did the photos in Gramps's album look so disappointing?

The thought of Gramps ushered in a wave of grief. He needed his wise counsel now more than ever. And he would ask him what he meant about seeing "where your hearts are." More words that teetered on the edge of discomfort.

Daniel turned on his heel at the end of the path to face a perfect panorama. His home sat perched on the cliff top, floor-to-ceiling windows bracketed by white boards and topped by gray slate. A symbol of success, to be paid for by his second book, the one Amanda was sure would cash in on the success of *No Secrets*.

Anxiety clawed at his neck. Who would take a photo of his book and scrub his name from the cover?

The gray clouds parted, and the white boards of his house glowed and throbbed in the afternoon sun. Daniel put the camera to his eye, but the brightness faded as if the clouds had joined again.

His finger closed down on the shutter but met resistance. There was no *clunk*. He squeezed the trigger again. Resistance. He checked the top of the camera. Next to the serrated silver knob was the tiniest window, and in it an angry, red *F*.

The film was used up. Again.

Someone had taken photos with the camera. Again.

Daniel breathed hard. This time it couldn't have been someone at work. It was either Milly or Kelly.

He tramped back to the house, annoyance growing with each step. It would cost him another thirty-three dollars to get this roll of film developed, and he *still* hadn't used the camera like Gramps wanted him to.

Daniel stared at his reflection in the polished floorboards of the foyer as if seeking strength in numbers. He would confront Kelly first.

The banging of cupboards drifted across the kitchen as he entered the hub of his home. Exposed Baltic pine beams stretched their way across the dining area to a series of white cupboards framed in gray. Their sheen caught the light from the full-length windows that opened onto their deck and the million-dollar view of the ocean. Kelly had stepped into this room and almost signed the contract on the spot. This kitchen could cater for three or three hundred.

Daniel composed himself as he pulled back a tall wicker chair from the counter and placed Gramps's camera in front of him.

Kelly looked at him over the remaining shopping bags. "How did the camera go?"

Daniel ordered the words in his mind. Restraint fought with frustration. Frustration won.

"I should ask you."

Confusion swept across Kelly's face. "What do you mean?"

The anger started its rise. "I took *a few* photos."

Kelly's brow wrinkled. "Okay."

Daniel clenched his hands, tired of the games. "But only a few because *someone* used the camera. *Again.*"

Kelly gasped. "Are you insinuating I used it? Because I didn't." She folded her arms. "And what do you mean *again?*"

Daniel scuffed his shoe against the chair leg. "You know that roll of film I thought was

Gramps's last photos? Well, it turns out someone at work used the camera instead."

"And what did they take photos of?"

"The other staff, but they were strange photos."

"How were they strange?"

Daniel handpicked his words with care. "Just not what you'd expect. People doing everyday things . . . although there was an upside. Whoever took the photos took one of Jade in tears. It turns out her father had just been told of his secondary cancer. So I could help."

"Well, that's a good thing, but why wouldn't the person who took the photo help her instead of taking her photo?"

"That's a question that's bothered me ever since I saw it. I thought we had a caring team, so that doesn't sit well with me."

"Who would do that?"

Daniel scratched the back of his neck. "I don't know. I asked around, but no one is owning up to it."

"So did someone at work use it again?"

"No, the camera has been home all this time." Practiced silence hung in the air to draw out an admission.

Kelly bristled. "I've told you I didn't. Have we reached a point where you don't believe me?"

"Well, it was either you or Milly."

Kelly sighed hard as she closed her eyes. Words deserted them, and a call on her cell phone broke the heavy silence that had settled on their standoff. She flicked a glance to the screen. "It's the school."

"Kelly Whiteley." She nodded in recognition. "Mrs. Kowalick. What can I do for you?"

Kelly's expression ebbed and flowed with the conversation. Quick nods, a painful squint with eyebrows clenched. There were few words, but her face said so much.

Daniel looked up the stairs at the closed door to Milly's bedroom. She had to have been the one who used the camera. He wrenched his gaze back to Kelly as she gasped, a hand over her mouth.

"Yes, we'll come and see you tomorrow after school." Another nod. "Yes, I'll make sure Milly is with us." A pained glance at Daniel. "Thanks for your call."

Kelly placed the phone gently on the counter, shock settling onto her face.

"That was Milly's teacher. She's worried about her because her marks are sliding toward failing grades."

Daniel's mind kicked into its analytical drive. So that explained Milly's withdrawal. She was struggling at school. Bad news, but good to know.

"Did you know about that, Daniel?"

He shook his head. "News to me, although it does explain why she's withdrawn into herself. And now I know how to talk to her."

Kelly folded defensive arms. "Don't push it on her, okay? For me? We're meeting at the school tomorrow, so I'd like to talk about it together."

"Whatever you like." Daniel's cogs continued to whir. Failing grades meant Milly's scholarship was under threat, and they couldn't afford fees at that academy *and* this house. "Her grades can't have fallen that far, can they? She needs to maintain a B average to keep the scholarship, so I'm glad the teacher nipped it in the bud. That's good news, at least."

Kelly's expression didn't agree as she slumped against the counter. "She's failing at school and couldn't talk to us about it?"

"It's okay. It doesn't matter how we found out. Now at least we know what to fix." Daniel looked up the stairs again, glad for a piece of the puzzle that would hopefully lift the first of the clouds that hung over their home.

Fourteen

S hame burned through the greasy, spidery strands of the young woman's hair, her face hovering inches from the toilet bowl.

Daniel moved to the next frame on Simon's wall. Why would someone allow that photo to be on display?

The next frame held a couple's altercation. A balding, ruddy man, his business shirt unbuttoned, stood with his arm around a young woman in a disheveled blouse. She clutched at his tie as if scrambling for a lifeline while a middle-aged woman in track pants and an orange San Francisco sweatshirt pulled at his arm, an angry sneer directed at her rival.

Daniel looked down the wall. While the photos were in sharp focus and dazzled with color, they were beyond embarrassing. A young woman caught mid-blink, cake falling from her overstuffed mouth. A man's leering grin, illuminated by his phone, his wife sound asleep beside him. A cloud of sharp, acrid chemicals tickled and then stung his nose. The smell of something developing.

Simon folded his white-gloved fingers as he stared into a small LED screen on the side of the blue-and-white processing machine. "They're nearly ready."

Daniel moved to the shelves on the opposite wall, the price tags hanging from the cameras fluttering at his approach. His finger flicked at the tag on the leather-concertinaed camera. "Fifteen hundred? This camera was ten thousand dollars last week. That's one heck of a discount."

"It's now the right price for the person who needs it."

"W.I.N.? What does that even mean?"

Simon smiled, his cheeks bathed in the faint glow of the LED. "Whatever Is Needed."

"So your cameras are for sale for either a set price or whatever is needed?"

"Yes, and most of the time 'Whatever Is Needed' is the higher price to pay."

Daniel shook his head in disbelief. "You must be new to business."

"This shop is new. I used to have another one not far from here." He clicked his fingers and then moved around the counter to the boxes under the shelves. "You'll need more film! Once you see the great clarity the Olympus HS-10 Infinity gives you, you'll want as many rolls as you can get." Simon pulled out a box filled to the brim with film canisters.

Not this again. "I haven't used the camera much yet. To be honest, the photos you produce are pretty disappointing." He waved a hand at the frames on the wall.

Simon stood and stroked his chin. "Why are they disappointing?"

"Have a look. People aren't smiling, and they look like they didn't even know the photo was being taken. I wouldn't put them in frames."

Simon's eyes glistened. "They have great clarity."

"Well, they are sharp, but they aren't great photos."

Disappointment clouded Simon's face. "So you can't see?"

"See what? These aren't the best photos of people at all."

Simon shook his head. "What if these are the moments that are the very definition of truth? The camera never lies, you know."

Daniel's pulse quickened. The phrase from Gramps's camera again.

A soft buzz came from the back of the lab. Simon drifted back to the processor as it spat photographs into its tray. He flicked through them, his fingertips tracing the images. "Just wonderful clarity." He placed them in an envelope and padded back to the counter.

Daniel held out his hand. "Thanks—"

Simon raised a finger and then reached under the counter, pulling out the roll of wax seal stickers. He delicately peeled one off and sealed the envelope. Then he held it out to Daniel in two hands and bowed his head. "It has been my pleasure to serve you."

In his hands Daniel held the answer to the question of whom he would confront at home.

"And a box of film?" Simon's plea rang over his shoulder.

Daniel dropped his head as his hand rested on the door handle. It wouldn't hurt to get another roll of film, just to save another visit. "Just one roll."

He turned, and Simon held one out for him. "When you bring this back, would you mind bringing in your grandfather's camera? I haven't seen the Infinity model in years."

Daniel pocketed the film canister and reached for his wallet. "Of course."

Simon held up his hand. "You take this one until you're ready for a box. You can learn so much even from just one roll of film."

Daniel headed for the door. There was movement in the corner of his eye, the slightest flutter of butterfly wings, as the little bell jingled his departure.

He peeled back the wax seal and steeled himself. He would be confronting either a wife who accused him of cheating or a daughter who didn't talk about anything.

In the first photo, clouds hung in brilliant, puffy white above an azure ocean, waves caught mid-pound over rocks shining emerald green. Along the walking path, flowers didn't so much bloom as threaten to burst through the photograph.

Simon was right about clarity.

He stopped short at the next photo. His own bedroom, pillows strategically placed on a made bed. The next photo, his living room, fashion magazines fanned over the coffee table next to fresh flowers. An invitation for a potential homeowner.

Daniel bit his lip. So it was Kelly, but was she preparing to sell the house? That was why she didn't want to own up to using Gramps's camera. She was preparing to leave him and sell the house. *That* explained her distance. A chill swept over him.

In the next photo, the purple and white pillows where Milly buried herself each night fronted her headboard, next to a nightstand on which sat her ever-present phone. Daniel squinted hard as he brought the picture closer. The glass on the framed family portrait next to her lamp was cracked. Angry scratches covered his face. And Kelly's.

Questions exploded in his head like fireworks. Why would Kelly see this and not tell him?

Daniel flicked to the next photo. A school report sat on their dining table. Across the top in Mrs. Kowalick's flowery handwriting was Milly's name, but the usual proud display of As didn't trail down the page. Instead, he saw a dirty flood of disappointing Ds and an occasional F. He was sure he hadn't seen this. He would remember grades this bad. That explained the phone call from the teacher, but why would Milly take a photo of this? Then a ray of revelation. She *had* reached out. She couldn't put the struggle into words, and this was the only way she could raise it with them. Somewhat relieved, Daniel's pace picked up. He held photos that wouldn't cause confrontation; they would provide the starting point for a solution.

Daniel skidded to a stop at the next photo. Kelly's suitcase sat next to their front door, and on it rested what looked like a letter or an invoice. A logo with a flash of purple was like the one on the bank statement in the photo he'd pulled from Gramps's recliner.

What else was Milly telling him through her anonymous photography?

Daniel's breath deserted him as he shuffled the final photo to the front. On his study desk sat a copy of *No Secrets*, his name again erased from the cover.

In its place, two initials.

His own.

Engraved on two cuff links.

Fifteen

The unforgiving plastic of Kelly's seat creaked as she shifted under the harsh fluorescence from overhead and a searchlight stare from Milly's teacher. Next time Milly said school wasn't much fun, she would agree.

The empty classroom filled with the slow tick of an aging second hand under the dusty face of the wall clock. A discordant player in a digital age.

A sixtysomething woman wrapped in a gray cardigan, her hair losing the battle against volume and control, tapped an impatient pencil on the desk as she glared over her half-moon glasses.

Kelly mimed taking out earbuds. Milly complied with a frown.

Mrs. Kowalick continued to tap. "I am surprised you waited for my call before coming in to talk about Milly."

Kelly looked across at her daughter, who looked away and stared out the window. "What do you mean?"

"The downward trend in Milly's grades is reflected in her report."

"Mrs. Kowalick, we haven't yet seen it."

Milly stared harder out the window.

The pencil froze mid-tap. "I see. Milly's work has always been of the highest standard—that's why we offered her the scholarship in the first place—but she is failing."

The chair next to Kelly creaked as Daniel threw an arm around Milly's shoulder. "Well?"

Kelly felt the outnumbering and stepped in. "Milly is coming to an age when things are changing and there's extra pressure on her."

Milly's eyes narrowed. Kelly would be unhappy, too, if she were spoken about as if she were a zoo exhibit.

Mrs. Kowalick straightened the pencil on her desk blotter. "I've got other students the same age in my class, Mrs. Whiteley, and their grades aren't slipping. Milly's are."

The slow ticks peeled away from the clock on the wall as Mrs. Kowalick laced thick fingers. "It's also her demeanor. I know girls can be on a roller coaster of emotion, but she seems more . . . flat than the others. That raised a red flag."

The news was a hammer blow to Kelly's maternal instinct. The depth of their disconnection was revealed when someone outside their family knew more about her daughter than she did.

"Mr. and Mrs. Whiteley, I don't mean to pry, but the welfare of one of my best students is at stake. Is everything okay at home?"

Daniel drummed his fingers harder on the back

114

of Milly's chair. "Like most families, we're under pressure, but we're working through it."

Kelly could feel Milly's eyes roll from two seats away.

Mrs. Kowalick's fierce eye contact locked on to her. "I'm more than happy to recommend the family to the school counselor—"

The electrical jolt of Daniel's cackle cut across the offer of help and bounced back from the whiteboard at the front of the classroom. "I'm not sure we need to go down that path."

Kelly's disappointment burned, fueled by the depth and speed of Daniel's reaction. Seeing someone was *exactly* what they needed to do.

Daniel smoothed his hands on his jeans. "Let's get down to the details. If Milly maintains her D average, will she lose her scholarship?"

Kelly flushed with a growing anger. D average? Daniel had seen Milly's report and not told her about it?

Milly stood up with a huff and stormed from the classroom, thumbing in her earbuds as she stomped into the corridor.

Mrs. Kowalick's gaze followed Milly from the classroom. "Yes, she will. I think you know she needs to maintain a B average."

Daniel stood, offering his hand. "I'll fix it. Thanks for your time." He hustled out of the room.

Kelly sat reeling, punch-drunk at the last

sixty seconds. She offered a weak smile as Mrs. Kowalick tapped her pencil in time with the ticking of the clock. She smiled back at Kelly, a closed smile that didn't include her eyes. "I will be keeping a close eye on Milly's grades over the next few weeks. I strongly suggest you have a word with her at home."

Nothing was worse than a lecture.

Kelly inspected the blooming red rose—the centerpiece of her platter of canapés—which fifteen minutes earlier had been a plain, simple tomato. She wished she could cut the unspoken tension with as deft a hand as she used to cater.

Daniel pushed past her and beelined for the fridge. Head down in focus, or something more than that? In the twenty-four hours since the meeting at school, Milly had resumed her silence. Daniel had closed down.

Kelly bit her lip. "Daniel?"

"Fourteen . . . fifteen . . . and three bottles of . . ." He looked over the open fridge door. "Yes?"

The tears welled. "Why didn't you tell me about her report card?"

Daniel closed the fridge and stroked his chin. "I presumed you'd seen it."

Kelly choked back an angry sob. "The first I knew about it was when you mentioned it to Milly's teacher. It was humiliating."

"I'm sorry, Kel. I thought you knew. I saw it just before we went to the school."

"Why would Milly just show you?"

Milly stood at the foot of the stairs, her phone held in front of her, the electronic shutter clicking away. Kelly forced a smile.

Daniel leaned back on the fridge. "Good timing, Mill. I've got a question for you. Why would you hide your report card?"

Two versions of her husband faced off right in front of Kelly. "I've got a question for you first, Dad. Since when do you go snooping through my locker at school?"

"I don't even know where your locker is."

"That's where I put my report card."

Daniel's eyes flicked around the room, a sure sign his steel-trap mind was twitching its razor-sharp teeth.

Milly's brow furrowed. "So how did you get into my locker?"

Daniel's voice rose. "I saw the photo you took with Gramps's camera, and your report card was sitting right on this kitchen counter."

Milly waved her phone. "Why would I use Gramps's camera when I've got this?"

Kelly watched back and forth at this tennis match of an exchange, lost as to where this conversation had come from—or was going. A shocked indignation showed on her daughter's face. Milly wasn't lying.

"And not only are you snooping but you're accusing me of stuff I haven't done!" She punched her earbuds back in and stormed up the stairs.

Kelly turned to Daniel. They needed to talk about this as a family. Calmly, not like this. "What is this about Gramps's camera?"

"I'm sorry. I accused you of using it, but it appears Milly did, and she took a photo of her report card. I thought it was her way of telling us about it."

"Why would she use Gramps's camera?"

"I don't know. Maybe because she knew I would see the photos. She took a few around the house, empty rooms and"—Daniel's gaze drifted to his shuffling feet—"a few other things."

"Why would she take photos of our house? And what other things?"

Daniel's voice slowed, as if he were measuring his words. "My cuff links from work." He stopped and then lifted his gaze to her. "And your suitcase next to the front door."

"My suitcase? Why?"

"I don't know. And some kind of bank statement. From a bank I'd never heard of until I found that photo in Gramps's recliner. Beyond Bank."

Kelly felt the blood drain from her face.

Sixteen

Daniel filled Anna's glass as the breeze swept across the deck. "Thanks so much for suggesting this celebration. I needed it more than I realized."

"Losing Gramps was difficult for you, and you've worked so hard since Howard passed away. You deserve it." As Anna took a sip, the breeze flicked the burgundy highlights across her face, the lowering sun kissing them with a deep-red glow.

Raucous laughter from his kitchen slipped under the glass doors and spilled outside. Comfortable silence descended on them, shepherded by the gentle breeze coming off the ocean. It felt like . . . a relief. Daniel batted away the feeling, his mind joining dots it didn't need to.

"Where's your better half?" he asked.

Anna nodded toward the kitchen. "In there, probably regaling your staff on the benefits of cloud computing. Kelly looks like she's having fun."

Through the doors, Kelly glided from group to group, platters of her afternoon's creation in each hand. "She's happy."

Daniel looked back from the kitchen and into Anna's glare, one eyebrow locked and loaded.

"Is she, Daniel? Really?"

"We have our problems like anyone, but Kelly still thinks I'm cheating on her. I don't know how to convince her I have done nothing wrong."

"Perhaps you need to look into why she doesn't believe you."

"Who knows? She's so defensive whenever we talk that it's almost like she doesn't want to be convinced. Anyway, my more pressing problem at the moment is Milly and her failing at school."

"How did the meeting with her teacher go?"

"Not well. It's frustrating to have answers my daughter won't let me give her. Honestly, it's much easier when the problems sitting in front of you belong to other families."

Anna laughed, her highlights now fiery, glowing embers in the setting sun. "I think that's what makes it harder for people like us to have the knowledge we do."

The gentle breeze ushered another wedge of comfortable silence onto the deck. The music roared as the glass doors to the deck flew open and Kelly sailed through, brandishing napkins and a fresh platter loaded with canapés, an intricate tomato rose at its center. A beaming smile gave way to tight lips, her eyes narrow and taut, a contrast to her free-flowing gray dress.

Anna took a napkin. "You've done a wonderful job with the food, Kelly. And you look gorgeous."

Kelly gave a slight bow. "Thanks. This dress might be old, but it still fits pretty well. Daniel said I've got you to thank for suggesting this dinner." She offered her the platter, rows of charred eggplant and salami and radish creations waiting for admiration as much as tasting. "So what are you two talking about out here?"

Daniel's eyes rolled skyward. *See?*

The edges of Kelly's mouth crinkled into a downward turn at the lack of an instant response, but then Peter barged onto the deck and into the gap where the conversation should have been. "So this is where the party is! Daniel, could I have a look at that camera now?"

"Sure, I think Milly might have it."

"Where is she?"

Daniel scanned the kitchen for signs of his daughter. "I don't know. I haven't seen her all afternoon . . ."

His sentence ran out of puff when he realized he was making the same mistake he'd made at her birthday party. "I'll find her."

Daniel charged into the house, Peter in tow, leaving Anna and Kelly with a platter and silence between them. He walked into the living room and a wall of soaring operatic strings and plaintive saxophone. No sign of Milly.

He felt a tug at his arm. Jade swayed as she

clutched a glass of wine, not her first, and she excused herself from a discussion with Cameron. "You've got a wonderful home, Daniel. You deserve to live in a million-dollar house like this."

Behind Daniel's embarrassed smile, the buzz of anxiety tickled through him as Jade unknowingly pried open the lid on his financial situation.

Peter leaned into the conversation with a wink. "You're right about the million-dollar bit!"

Jade laughed. "Well, you deserve it, and I'm grateful for your insight."

Daniel smiled. "How *is* your father?"

"Touch and go. But your words last week were perfectly timed. I still don't know how you noticed."

Someone had noticed before him. The someone who took Jade's photo. "It's what we do at Crossroads, notice when people are struggling and do something about it. Didn't anyone else see you upset?"

Peter's face remained stony blank.

Jade furrowed her brow. "No."

Someone *must* have. "Are you sure?"

Jade drained her glass. "No. Just you."

Daniel set his jaw. "I hope your father is feeling better soon. Enjoy the evening."

He headed toward his study as Peter's question arrived over his shoulder. "I only knew about it when she told me. How *did* you know?"

Daniel stuck his head into his study. There was no sign of Milly, but Gramps's camera sat on his desk, and he handed it to Peter. "Would you mind taking photos of the evening?"

"Sure, happy to." He wandered back toward the noise.

Daniel moved to the kitchen. Someone *had* noticed Jade but *not* done something about it. Then a polite knock at the front door cut through his thickening thoughts and the soaring music.

When Daniel opened the door, his breath jammed in his throat. Monique stood in the half-light, a black dress hugging every curve down to her calves, a sparkle on her neck, her hair up save for two tendrils that fell on either side of thick lashes and wide eyes. A heady waft of Chanel threatened to derail his marriage on the spot. Monique's smile eased into his discomfort.

He scrambled to regain a sense of control and stepped back to breathe distance into their interaction. "Monique, welcome! May I get you a drink?" He waited for the inevitable. It didn't take long.

Daniel felt Kelly arrive behind him five seconds before he heard her voice. "Hello, and welcome to our family home." She thrust a fresh platter between them. "Something to eat?"

Kelly's voice hardened as she turned to Daniel. "A few people need drinks. I suggest you fill them." She turned back to Monique. "Please come in and enjoy the evening."

Daniel was pleased for the escape route—and the chance to avoid giving Kelly ammunition she didn't need.

Peter raced up to him, brandishing the camera. "This is wonderful. It has a unique quality to it when you look through the viewfinder."

"Would you use the word *clarity?*"

Peter waved a finger. "Yes! I've never seen a camera like it, and like I said, I've had some Olympus cameras over the years."

Daniel felt fingers on his arm, pulling him toward the deck. Monique, holding a champagne flute.

"Daniel, can we talk?" Her glass was empty. Already.

Daniel planted his feet. "Sure."

Monique gestured to the deck. "Alone?"

A faint alarm sounded in his head, and his testosterone fought to hit snooze on it. "Can't we talk here?"

Monique's head tilted, baited lashes batting. "Please? For just a moment?"

A moment. He could give one of his own staff members a moment. Monique's curves sashayed across the deck toward the railing. Daniel forced his eyes to stay on the back of her head. She spun to face him, the playful breeze bouncing her curls on flushed cheeks. "I just want to thank you for the opportunity you've given me to work at Crossroads."

That had to be said on the deck, alone? The alarm bell rang louder. It was time to put an end to this. Here. Maybe *that* would be enough for Kelly. "It's great to have you on the team." Daniel moved to the door.

"Daniel?"

His rational side screamed at him to head back inside, but the buzz of his hormones pulled rank. "Yes?"

"We make a great team. Two couples said today we've saved their marriage."

His self-control was losing the battle as the sun lowered behind Monique, the breeze bouncing those tendrils. His testosterone pumped his heart harder and threw his brain out of the ring, but then his professionalism tagged in and reminded him of the red flag flickering in the same breeze that rustled Monique's hair. But then over the top, his indignation kicked in. This was *his* house.

Monique leaned back on the railing and crossed her ankles, a thin line of gold catching his eye. "By the way, I've got news about the friend I told you about. She's decided that if she's found the right man for her, she'll do something about it."

Daniel threw a glance over his shoulder at the happy team enjoying his happy home. Indignation or not, there was a price to pay, and it was too high. He reached deep into his well of self-control to save his future from the mire.

"This friend of yours should talk to someone if she needs some formal advice. I have to get back to my guests."

Monique smiled. Those ruby-red lips. Her eyes flicked over Daniel's shoulder, and his eyes followed hers. Kelly stood openmouthed, half-empty platter in hand.

"Daniel, can I get your help inside at your own function, please?" A staccato monotone, flint in her voice, quavering with seething anger.

"Yes. We were just finishing up." His mind arranged the cue cards it would need for tomorrow's inevitable defense.

Monique's voice floated over his shoulder. "Daniel is just enjoying himself . . . at his own function."

Kelly marched past Daniel, first thrusting the platter into his chest. She stood in front of Monique, hands on hips, a living, breathing example of what the psychology textbooks referred to as an attack position. He had to step in.

"Kelly, nothing was—"

Kelly breathed ragged and hard. "Listen here. You think you have something Daniel wants, but you will not break up my home or my marriage."

Monique sagged for a moment but then stood tall in defiance. "That's Daniel's decision, isn't it?" Her champagne glass gripped in trembling fingers, she shouldered past Kelly.

Daniel dropped his head. "When we don't have a houseful of guests, I will tell you what did—and did not—happen. We need to talk about this."

Kelly looked out at the low sun, a golden thumbprint in a reddening sky. "We need to talk about a lot of things. I want us to see someone. Together."

"Well, for the sake of our guests, can we just put it to one side and talk about it tomorrow?"

A timer beeped in the kitchen—a siren call to a caterer—and Kelly stormed back into the house.

Daniel stewed in frustrating bitterness. He had handled Monique well, but the same phrase screamed at him on a loop from deep within. *I have done nothing wrong.* But Kelly would never buy it.

At the far end of the deck, something moved behind the barrel grill. Milly swung her feet while perched on the railing. She had seen everything.

"Milly, would you get down from there, please?"

Her defiant legs swung harder. "If you can't get along, can't you at least pretend?"

Daniel closed his eyes and breathed hard through his nose. "I think it's good if the people at work see a couple working through their issues."

Milly jumped down and stood tall as she drilled a glare into her father. "I was talking about for me."

The brilliant reds and oranges of the sunset bathed Daniel in a warm glow as they rebounded from the full-length glass doors. He wished he could copy and paste this moment in time—a happy and successful team, laughter filling his dream home.

Peter pushed the remnants of his black forest cake into the middle of the large redwood table. "Wonderful cake, Kelly. You were right—the second piece was better."

Peter's long-suffering wife elbowed him as he guffawed at his own joke.

Kelly bowed as a wave of compliments swept across the table. Black crumbs and dots of cream trailed from the remains of her creation in the table's center to the happy, now satisfied, team from Crossroads Counseling.

As Daniel surveyed the tableau of satisfaction and happy chatter, a dark shadow passed over him. The dark days of Howard's passing. The quick plunge into bad health and the shock of his diagnosis. The mounting pressure from the bank to keep the practice open. Cleaning out Howard's office inside a month. Saving a practice and his future.

He stood as Peter clinked his glass with a

chocolate-smeared spoon and a hush fell over the group.

"I want to say thank you to the team not just from me but on behalf of all the couples who have come through our doors."

There was a smattering of applause. Daniel looked across the remnants of the cake at Anna and smiled.

"You know, one thing is common to everyone who comes to Crossroads Counseling, and it's not that they want to meet Peter Gardner—"

Peter raised his hands in mock protest as laughter broke out around the table.

"—it's that they know we can help."

Kelly looked up at him, fierce pride in her eyes. The truce was holding.

"We have a great team here, almost family." Monique beamed at him, and Daniel glanced away into the reflected sunset. "After Howard died, I thought the practice wouldn't survive. In the last months of his life, Howard spent more time hunched over his computer than counseling, and the business was looking dire."

He saw tears forming in Anna's eyes as she held her husband's hand.

"We have just helped our thousandth couple. Howard set us on our path, and he gave us a gift to share with everyone. He was more than a mentor; he was the catalyst to everything we do. He established Crossroads Counseling and then employed me—the second great thing he did."

A harsh, over-the-top cackle burst from Monique. Heat from Kelly radiated at his elbow.

"Now we're one of the most recognizable practices in the city, thanks to a little book you all know."

Milly slouched in a chair on the far side of the deck. He had lost the battle but won a compromise. She wouldn't sit at the table, but she was screenless.

"Everyone who has played a key role at Crossroads is here tonight." Daniel raised his glass. "So I would like to toast Howard Jones, Crossroads Counseling, and the thousandth couple who came to us for help, but most importantly, I would like to raise a glass to all of you."

The air thundered with cheers and the clinking of glasses. Kelly looked up at him with a smile, and in that moment of connection, Daniel was transported back to happier times, to the moment he came home and told her Howard wanted him, fresh out of grad school armed with his master's in counseling. She had joked that being married to a counselor should mean they would never need therapy.

Anna stood as she dabbed away tears. "Thank you, Daniel. Your leadership is the backbone of our success. It's more than the book. It's also your integrity and strength of character."

As she raised her glass again, Daniel felt the slightest twinge of discomfort. The faint whisper of a memory long buried.

Anna wasn't finished. "I'd like to suggest a memento to remind us of tonight—something permanent. Maybe a group photo we could hang in our reception area to celebrate everyone who has helped us succeed?"

Daniel called Milly over. "Would you mind?"

Milly slunk over to the table and picked up Gramps's camera.

The jostling started as chairs were pushed back and the group moved to the railing. Peter stood front and center of them, and Jade moved to hide at the back despite her lack of height. Spouses not on the front lines of couple therapy shuffled to one side.

Anna directed traffic as she shoved Peter out of the way. "We need Daniel in the center."

Kelly moved in next to Daniel. Monique barged past her to stand on his other side, and Daniel felt Kelly's protective arm slide around his waist.

Peter clicked his fingers. "Anna, you were there in the beginning, so you need to be in the middle next to Daniel." Monique stood her ground as Anna approached but then reluctantly ceded her turf. Anna squeezed in next to Daniel.

Kelly released her grip as Anna bunched in closer, and Daniel was sandwiched between the two women who had played such a big part in his life.

A fierce sunset radiated from the doors behind Milly. This would be a great photo; a fine recognition of everyone who played a role in the success of Crossroads Counseling.

With a chunky *click* and a blinding flash, Milly took the photo.

As the team moved away, Daniel stared into the warmth of the reflection and the one part of his life that was going well.

Peter leaned forward. "Um, we're finished, you two."

Embarrassed, Daniel stepped away from Anna, who shook her head as if shaking herself back to the present.

Seventeen

The steam rose from the dim sims as Daniel cut them with his fork. Above him red-and-yellow paper lanterns swung in the crisp, conditioned air, nudging dark-brown bamboo screens that flanked a large fish tank. A long, gray catch of the day glided back and forth for its final few minutes as it surveyed its likely predators. Today there were just two.

"It's nice to be able to unload after last night."

Anna placed her chopsticks on the steaming bowl in front of her. "You know how we promised we'd have each other's back? I saw the tension between you and Kelly, and I'm sure you're dealing with that, but I also saw what happened with Monique."

With a loud sigh, Daniel laced his fingers behind his head. This was already a long day after a bad start, a morning rush under attack with visual daggers and staccato questions from Kelly, unaccepting of his explanations of innocence over what didn't happen on the deck.

"What you do in your own life is up to you, Daniel. But when it becomes a work issue, I have to speak up. I want to talk to you as a friend as much as a colleague."

Daniel lifted a whole dim sim into his mouth to give his thoughts some time to develop.

"I put my foot down with Monique and asked her to talk to someone about her issues. Isn't that enough?"

Anna's eyebrow ratcheted up. "You need to be clearer about where the boundary is."

Daniel fought the urge to slam his chopsticks onto the table. "Nothing happened!"

"Come on. You know this better than I do. Monique has interpreted your lack of a no as a yes."

Where there should have been more anger was instead relief at hearing it out loud. His eyes drifted to the fish tank. The fish swam back and forth, forth and back. "I'll talk to her."

"And if you need someone to talk to about your marriage issues—together or alone—I'm here for you."

Daniel reached for another prawn cracker. "I'm not sure Kelly would come to Crossroads, let alone to see you."

"I realize that, but I can also see how your credibility could be undercut if you're seen visiting a marriage counselor. I thought you might like to keep it in-house."

Daniel studied his business partner in admiration. She understood him.

Anna's eyebrow raised. "I've known you for years, so I know you can't help fixing things. Plus, you're a guy."

"Thanks for noticing."

Anna smirked. "And a proud one at that. You realize marriage counselors aren't immune from relationship problems? Maybe you need to take some time to talk things through."

Time. A rare commodity. "I can't take time off. I'm under pressure to finish this book, which will take a whole heap of pressure off. I need to put my head down and get through it. Taking a break now will just make it look like I can't cope."

Still Anna's eyebrow stayed aloft. "Now you sound like the men who sit in my office. You might be a bestselling author and hotshot counselor, but you're still a guy."

Their laughs interlaced across the table, and Anna slurped up another noodle. "I'm excited to see that group photo. It just felt right to capture that moment when everyone who has contributed to our success was there."

A short Chinese man with a food-smeared black apron wandered to their table. "Is everything to your satisfaction?"

Daniel patted a full stomach. "As always, Mr. Ming, your food is incredible. But we'll take the check now."

"Must be a working lunch today? No time for partners?" Their chef offered a saucy wink, laid the check on the table, and then, after a deep bow, continued his stroll around the empty tables in his restaurant.

Anna wiped her mouth with a napkin. "Interesting timing that a film processing shop opens just as you're given that camera."

"Just lucky, I guess."

Anna leaned across the table. "I know you want to put the counseling to one side, but I had a chat with Milly last night."

Daniel stopped pulling his wallet out of his trousers. "Did she say anything about what's bothering her?"

"Yes."

Thank goodness. "It's school, isn't it?"

"No, home. She told me a few things that she asked me not to share, but I'd be happy to talk with her further."

Daniel's nod grew with his relief. "I can't get through to her, so anybody talking to Milly would be great."

Simon's comment bounced around Daniel's head as he walked back to the car.

The dinner looked like it was the start of something special.

But it wasn't Simon's strange words that troubled Daniel. When he'd pressed Simon for an explanation for his intrusion, the evangelical zeal in his faraway eyes, the shine on his cheeks, and the broadness of his grin bothered him. It was bad enough Simon had charged him forty-four dollars this time, saying something about that was the price to pay. Still, it wouldn't ruin his day. He had a solution for Milly's problems— Anna. Kelly would have to agree with that.

Daniel whistled on his way to the car. He tore the wax seal sticker and riffled through the photographs, his breath held for any nasty surprises.

There weren't any. His staff enjoying the party, his own home, the celebration dinner on the deck . . . Daniel heaved a sigh of relief as he got into his car and threw the envelope onto the passenger seat before roaring off. He tapped the steering wheel, the haze in his mind clearing for the first time in a long while. Anna was right. Taking a moment to celebrate was important. He'd come a long way since Howard's death.

A traffic light dropped into amber, and he pulled up to red. He reached for the envelope. Cameron had a supportive arm around Jade. Monique blew a kiss with a saucy wink at the camera.

Green light.

Daniel put down the envelope as he accelerated. He now had a defense for Monique's behavior. He hadn't taken her photo, so she was blowing a kiss to Peter—she was like that with everyone. She wasn't zeroing in on him.

Amber slid to red. The next photos showed his staff on the deck, laughing in one another's company, glasses raised and heads thrown back. But behind them was a figure, arms waving in the air. Daniel squinted. Milly stood on the railing, her arms outstretched as if ready to swan dive to the rocks two hundred feet below. A creeping horror swept over him. Milly's cry for attention was unnoticed by everyone, including him. Again.

Daniel flicked to the next photograph. Kelly stared out the open front door into the night. Sure, she had stormed off the deck, but why would she allow Peter to take a photo like that?

Green light.

The residue of suspicion clung to him as he drove on. Why would Peter even want to take a photo of Kelly like that? It was like seeing Gramps's photo album . . .

The haze swirled back across his thoughts. The photos in Gramps's album were of people at the wrong moment, except that moment turned out to mean something. Gramps and his betting slip. Daniel and Kelly together but alone on the sofa. Milly in tears at her party.

So what did Kelly's photo mean? He shook his head. Now he was wondering what all the photos meant.

Amber. Daniel slowed and stopped at red. His team sat around the table enthralled with his speech, drinking in his heartfelt thanks for being part of the success of Crossroads Counseling. But in the corner of one photo, just under his elbow, someone was not enthralled. Above folded arms,

Kelly's eyes rolled, boredom writ large on her face.

Green light.

Daniel fumed as he sped away. So much for a truce. He had tried, bringing up issues in the right way, fighting to keep his professional knowledge at bay, hard as it was.

Daniel slowed as he pulled up to another red light.

Two photos left. Kelly's suitcase stood next to the front door. Balancing on it was a piece of paper emblazoned with the purple logo of that bank he'd never done business with. Daniel remembered welcoming people to his home, and her suitcase wasn't there then. He closed his eyes and breathed hard. She needed to talk to someone, but she wanted to go to counseling only if she picked the professional, and he couldn't afford for that to happen. He would just have to talk her into seeing Anna.

Daniel pulled the last photo from the envelope. The group photo, to be enlarged and hung proudly in the reception area at Crossroads. The oranges and reds of the sunset burned behind the group, on every face a sharp smile for the camera.

But one face wasn't looking at the camera.

A sinking feeling built in the pit of his stomach. He stood next to his wife, but Anna was looking up at him, a glistening admiration in her eyes, a beaming smile on her lips.

But what he saw next stopped his heart.

He was holding hands.

With Anna.

What on earth was this? He had *not* done that; he was sure. Or *had* he, without knowing? His mind scrambled, whisked by doubt. Had he? He was sure he hadn't!

Sweat beaded on his brow. He had promised to hang this photo at Crossroads, but there was no way he could allow that now.

His eyes drifted to the right-hand side of the photograph, past the entire group that Daniel had toasted for the success of Crossroads Counseling.

Another figure was in the photo.

Standing next to Peter was an old man, hair graying around his temples and flowing behind him, a hippie frozen in time. The thick black glasses perched on the end of his nose and the sparkle in his eyes were unmistakable.

A chill swept through Daniel.

His mentor. The founder of Crossroads.

Howard Jones.

Howard clasped a thick sheaf of dog-eared papers, with two big, black, chunky words on the front page.

No Secrets.

Beneath that, three smaller words: *by Howard Jones*.

Green light.

Flashes of light fired behind Daniel's eyes.

Howard held the manuscript Daniel had found in his desk just after he passed away.

Green light.

The driver behind him leaned on his horn. It was time to move.

But Daniel was going nowhere.

Eighteen

Kelly nestled into the sofa cushions in the living room she loved, her phone to her ear, her tablet teetering on her knees. Her finger flicked the news story up and down, down and up, its screaming headline burned not into the screen but into her conscience.

Dozens of children hooked up to ECG machines because of medication. The story didn't mention Rubicon Pharma. It didn't need to.

"I can't be a part of this anymore, Jasmine."

Jasmine's response didn't even register. Kelly's eyes drifted from the pebbles stacked in the glass vase that matched the lampshades she'd spent hours selecting to the whitewash of the cabinets to the flowers daubing color around the room. The expanse of the kitchen, its marble counter not a work surface but a palette for a caterer. She couldn't lose this place. Until Daniel's second book came out, they could cut some financial corners. Sell her car. Reduce the budget somehow. Just for a few months.

"—and then we'll find out there were never any problems."

"I wish I had your confidence, Jas. Every time

I hear Gascon explain all this away, I'm more convinced Mendacium is dangerous."

"I'm sorry you feel that way, but I'll keep going until I hear we've got a serious problem with it. Ignorance is bliss and all that."

"The saying I can't get out of my head is that ignorance is no excuse." She couldn't afford for this to eat away at her until she had nothing left.

An extra beat of silence came from Jasmine's end of the conversation, pregnant with intent.

"What?"

"You know I love you, but if you were so hot on ignorance, you wouldn't be pretending your husband isn't replacing you with his receptionist."

Her suspicions had been all but confirmed at the dinner when Daniel's words claimed there was nothing to worry about and yet the corners of Monique's lacquered lips said otherwise. Her self-esteem leaped forward and mugged her. Daniel was stringing along a younger version of her at his work. She had tried hard—for herself, for her employer, and for her husband—to look like the woman she'd once been, but the weight kept creeping back, the lines on her face first appearing and then deepening.

"Kel, remember what I said about leaving him? Maybe now's the time to play that card."

Tears filled Kelly's eyes as her future flashed before her. A world of pain. The house she loved carved down the middle. Milly would go with her, but she would be a reminder of Daniel, Daddy's little princess. How had she come to this point? She was married to a marriage counselor, for crying out loud! How on earth could this happen with everything Daniel knew? With the advice he gave to everyone else?

"I need to confront him, but what's the point? He's denied everything so far, so I need evidence."

The front door flew open, and Daniel staggered into the foyer.

"Gotta go. Daniel's home."

"Good luck. And don't forget to be strong—"

Kelly scrambled to sit up as she cut the call. "What happened? Are you okay?"

Daniel stared right through her. "Um, yeah, okay, I guess—"

"I need to talk to you about work, but you look like you need to talk more than me."

Daniel stared over her into the kitchen, his eyes glazed as he frowned and blinked, blinked and frowned. "I don't even—"

He snapped out of it and fixed a gaze on Kelly. "What do you need to talk about?"

Kelly reeled at the sharp change in direction. She couldn't just jump in and talk about quitting her job. She had to lead up to it.

"These news stories about Mendacium won't go away. Children are now in the hospital in agony with headaches my product has probably caused. I can't keep going if children will suffer after I've told their doctors they'll be fine."

"Can you confirm the side effects are real?"

"I've tried, but instead of answers I get motivation."

A slow nod from Daniel. "So there are side effects."

"Almost certainly." Kelly took a deep breath and plunged into the deep end of the conversational pool. "I need to think about whether I quit. I can't be part of this." Kelly studied Daniel's eyebrows. They remained unknotted. Hallelujah.

Daniel sat down on the edge of the sofa. "I don't want you to do this long term if it will keep you awake at night."

An old connection flickered to life. They were on the same page after months of not even being in the same story. "We'll need to rearrange a few things—maybe sell my car, reduce the budget—but it's only for a few months until your next book comes out."

Knots rippled in Daniel's jaw, and he strode to the kitchen, the distance between them yawning back into place. "It may be longer than that."

Kelly reeled as their disconnection yawned back into place. "Why is it taking so long?"

Daniel spun on his heel, his raised voice making her jump. "Because it is! It's not so easy to come up with another book."

Well, that was an overreaction. She would have to calm him down before raising the issue of the receptionist. "I'm sorry if I upset you. I just thought it would be easy because *No Secrets* was."

Daniel flushed a deep red. "Well, it wasn't, okay?" He stomped around the kitchen, slamming cupboards until he found a glass. "One day it came to me."

Kelly shrank back on the sofa. Daniel's anger had made occasional appearances, but this time it was as if she'd not just touched a nerve but sliced it open.

"Don't yell at me if you're upset. I said I was sorry—"

Daniel bustled over to the sofa and slid in next to her, looming over her with a menace she'd never seen in him. Ever. "Do you not trust me to write a book? Is that what you're saying?"

That straw broke the back of Kelly's tolerance. A flood of hurt poured out in a gush. "Trust? You spend the evening on the deck with your receptionist in her painted-on cocktail dress all the while claiming nothing is going on despite her challenging me to my face. You work late at the office, only coming home when I call wondering where you are. You are in no position to talk about trust!"

Daniel closed his eyes and growled through his teeth. *"I have done nothing wrong!* What will it take for you to accept that?" His cell phone pinged, and he grimaced as he checked it before turning it facedown on the sofa.

"I know what I saw on the deck, Daniel. And to be honest, doing the right thing is not as simple as avoiding the wrong thing."

Daniel shook exasperated tears from his eyes. "What more can I do?"

That was better. "I need to know you've drawn a line through anyone else."

"I have."

"So I've got nothing to worry about at Crossroads?"

"No, you haven't. And frankly, I'm tiring of saying it."

"And what I saw at the work dinner was nothing to worry about?"

"No."

Now was the time. "We need to see someone."

Daniel shrugged. "Can't we just talk?"

"That's the problem. I want to talk to my husband, not a counselor."

Daniel thought about it for a moment. "Fair enough. We can talk about seeing someone else. There are some things I'd like to know too."

A truce settled between them. More a cease-fire than peace.

Daniel calmed as he breathed hard through his nose. "Something happened at the work dinner you need to know about."

A numbness washed over Kelly. Hadn't he just said nothing happened?

"It's Milly."

Kelly traded her suspicion and self-defense for a sinking sense of failure. "What happened?"

"Milly was trying to get people's attention by threatening to jump from the railing of our deck."

Kelly's hand shot to her mouth. "Who saw her?"

Daniel started his sentence before reeling it in and having a second go at it. "It doesn't matter. What matters is that Milly talked with someone about her problems."

"It doesn't matter? And what do you mean she's talked with someone?"

Daniel beamed. "Anna, and she's offered to talk more with her."

The relief in Kelly clashed with an expected self-defense. Daniel had turned to his work-wife to fix their daughter. She shrugged to keep the tension in her shoulders from creeping up her neck and broadcasting its presence across her face. She failed.

"Anna is a trained counselor, and our daughter turned to her. At least she turned to someone." He leaned away from her. "Or is this about something else?"

The last of the connection that had sparked back to life fizzled and then faded. Then a heavy silence.

Milly padded down the stairs, removing her earbuds on the final steps. Kelly didn't need her daughter to see them fighting. Again. Not after the breakthrough of Milly finally talking to someone. Anyone. She had to deflate the tension, so she turned to Daniel. "Did you get the photos from the work dinner?"

Daniel stiffened. "They're at work."

"Any good ones?"

"I think so." Daniel stood from the sofa and disappeared into the study.

Kelly stared at the closing door. Why the gear shift to disinterest? What was in the photos he didn't want her to see? It had to have something to do with what happened on the deck. Even after his denials.

Daniel's phone pinged. With a sideways glance at Milly, who was shoulder-deep in the fridge, Kelly grabbed it and headed out to the deck.

The text message was from a woman but not one from work. Amanda, his editor. "Daniel, we've all but lost the momentum we had with *No Secrets*. It's been nearly a year now. Call me."

Kelly threw a furtive glance back into the house. Milly still grazed in the fridge. Daniel's study door remained closed.

She back-arrowed to the list of her husband's messages. Before Amanda's message was a recent text from an unknown number. Five minutes ago, when he'd turned over his phone.

"Daniel, we need to talk at work tomorrow. Mon." Then a second message, almost as an afterthought: "xx."

Kelly fought hard to rein in an anguished scream and swept away the message with a quivering finger. She had her evidence. If Daniel didn't mention anything after tomorrow's workday, something was going on. And he was lying. She needed to know where he got these photos developed. Her finger flicked through his phone history. No unfamiliar but persistent phone numbers. No calendar entries. And nothing about the photos.

Kelly reentered the kitchen, vindicated but grubby. How had her marriage reached a point where she was snooping through her husband's phone messages? Silently, she placed his phone on the counter.

Milly closed the fridge, a block of cheese in hand. "Do you snoop in my stuff like you do with Dad's?"

"I was just checking the details of Dad's photo place. Do you know where he takes Gramps's camera film?"

"No, but he said Monique from work found a place."

So the answer to the question of Daniel's faithfulness lay with the receptionist who wanted him to break it.

Nineteen

Daniel couldn't shake the image of Howard appearing on his deck, three years after he'd delivered the eulogy at his funeral. Howard did *not* appear on his deck. Howard *could* not appear on his deck. And he *hadn't* been holding hands with Anna.

There was only one explanation: Simon. He was manipulating his photos to blackmail him. Another situation to fix, but this one was easy. He would go there after his next appointment and threaten legal action. But there was one question he couldn't answer, one that led him deeper into the murky waters of possible blackmail. If Simon knew the truth about *No Secrets*, then he was working with someone Daniel knew.

But who? Another counseling practice? Simon said he'd had another shop. Maybe it was near Flinders Counseling, Peter's old practice, still smarting over Daniel's poaching of their brilliant young counselor. Or was this Kelly's way of forcing him to see someone? He needed to know who knew. And once he found out, he needed to shut them down. If he didn't, he'd be laughed out of counseling as a fraud, and once the media got wind of it, they'd camp in front of his house until they had dragged his name through the mud.

Anna's burgundy highlights swung through his office door. "Hey, Boss!"

Daniel tried to raise a smile and failed. His second attempt was more successful.

Anna cocked her head. "How did the group photo turn out?"

Daniel concentrated hard to keep the manufactured smile from falling from his lips. "Uh, there was a . . . problem with it at the photo place." That much was true.

"That's a shame. Make sure you fix it so we can hang it in the reception area."

Daniel had to shift the conversation. "Could you send in Monique? I need to chat with her."

Anna's eyebrow stayed aloft as she disappeared into the corridor. A moment later, Monique came into his office and shut the door. She perched on the edge of the sofa.

Daniel took a deep breath as he plowed into the speech he'd rehearsed on the drive into work. "Monique, I'm sorry if you've taken my friendship the wrong way. You are a wonderful young woman whose professionalism I respect. You make a difference to Crossroads and our clients. But I need you to understand that the level of our relationship is strictly professional."

Satisfied he'd delivered his message, he sat back, ready to pick up the pieces.

"No."

Daniel was prepared for a storm of tears. He wasn't prepared for "No."

"What do you mean, no?"

Monique looked up at Daniel from beneath those eyelashes. "She makes you unhappy, Daniel. I will make you happy."

Daniel shoved his testosterone down. Way down. "Monique, it can't be that way."

The thin veneer of Monique's bravado cracked. Her bottom lip dropped, then her eyes, and then the tears.

"I think it's just—"

"You can't do this to me!" Monique stood in a rush, and the door banged hard into the arm of his couch as she stormed out.

Daniel closed his eyes as his pulse thumped in his ears. He was being a case study in how to stay true to his marriage vows, unlike the men who filtered through his counseling door, eyes glued to the carpet or defiant in a firmer-than-normal handshake.

He needed air before his next appointment. Daniel grabbed his phone and headed down the corridor, running headlong into Peter.

"Great dinner the other night!"

"Thanks, Pete. It was . . ." Daniel's indignation needed an outlet. "Hey, thanks for taking a photo of Milly standing on the railing and not telling me."

Peter's gaze probed him. "I never saw Milly on the railing. I can assure you that if I had, I would have told you."

Daniel backpedaled. "Sorry. I've just had an uncomfortable but necessary conversation with Monique."

"Is everything okay?"

"It is now." Daniel moved past Peter and headed for some fresh air.

Peter's voice came from over his shoulder. "If I didn't take a photo of Milly on the railing, who did? Could you show me the photo?"

No, he couldn't. Showing Peter Milly's photo would lead to the group photo.

Monique's desk was empty. The reception area wasn't.

"Daniel!"

Laurie Wood jumped to her feet, hand extended. "Sorry if we're a bit early, but it's so nice of you to greet us out here." She pumped his hand. "You are a miracle worker. Well, your book is."

Daniel edged back from the wave of enthusiasm Laurie was surfing. He nodded to a smiling Mark on the couch, sitting under the empty space on the wall where there should have been a large photo of the Crossroads Counseling team.

"It's just an amazing book. How did you jam so much great counseling advice in there?"

Daniel tried to shut out her voice so he could

think. "It's difficult to do, Laurie . . . Why don't you head down to my office—"

But Laurie's wave was just cresting. "Saying you've got to be open. If your partner is offering help, it's proof they care—just wonderful! I've already read it twice and told everyone on Facebook your next book will blow them away! When is it coming out?"

Laurie's stabbing bursts of praise pierced his conscience. He wasn't the oracle she claimed him to be.

Daniel ushered the couple down the corridor. He needed to keep his head in the game, and then, after he'd shown them the door, he would confront Simon.

Daniel closed the door on Mark and Laurie and picked up Gramps's camera.

The engraving on its base flashed in the light. *No matter what you think you might see, the camera never lies.* Daniel's fingers probed the lens, the trigger, the back of the camera . . . No one had tampered with it. He pulled the group photo from his satchel. Howard stood to the side of the group, clutching his manuscript. Guilt trumped Daniel's sadness at seeing Howard.

It had to be Photoshop.

Daniel twisted the photo in the light, examining the edges of Howard's figure for clues. But that just raised a more serious question: How did Simon know about Howard?

Daniel placed the envelope and camera in his satchel and threw it over his shoulder. Head down, he charged into the corridor . . . and into Peter.

"Daniel, do you have a moment?"

"If you're quick."

"Why won't you show me the photo of Milly?"

Daniel slammed a door on the answer. He couldn't afford to be analyzed by a mind as sharp as Peter's.

"Obviously, I got my wires crossed. Don't worry about it."

"If you say so." Peter stroked his chin, studying Daniel. "Actually, no. I don't think I've ever seen your wires crossed before. What's going on?"

Daniel didn't know, but he was about to find out.

Twenty

T he harsh chirp of the dial tone sliced through the thumping of the pulse in Kelly's ear. She closed the doors to the house from the deck, the scene of her confrontation with the woman about to take her call.

"Hello. Welcome to Crossroads Counseling!" The spring in the receptionist's voice almost pronounced her punctuation.

"Good morning, Monique. It's Kelly. Kelly Whiteley."

The spring uncoiled. "Oh, hi."

"Is Daniel available?"

"He left the office about ten minutes ago."

A light breeze flitted off the ocean. Kelly's pulse thudded on. Time for a long shot. "I need your help."

Monique's silence was loud.

"Daniel has asked me to pick up his photos, but I didn't write down the place he said I should go."

"Maybe I should pick them up for Daniel."

Kelly cringed at the way her husband's name sounded coming out of her mouth. It stoked her anger into flame. "That's fine, Monique. I can do it."

"I'm happy to run errands for Daniel, if that's what he needs."

The flame flared higher. "Could you put me through to Anna?"

Monique all but chuckled. "She's out too. Listen, the photo place is just around the corner, so it would make more sense if I picked them up for him."

Just around the corner . . . Bingo! That had to be the bank of mom-and-pop shops that had survived the crushing corporate jackboot of megamalls and global brands. The home of Ming's Court Chinese Restaurant, where Kelly and Daniel had celebrated each tiny milestone in the early days of Crossroads with to-die-for steamed dim sims.

"Thanks, Monique." Kelly cut the call with more than a little relish.

A tiny bell jingled and a thick curtain of acrid chemicals stung Kelly's nose, firing memories of her high school photography class, of the first creative expressions on film and fumbles in the darkroom.

A young man with slicked-back silver hair stood behind the counter. Kelly approached him, a wall of antique cameras to her right, a jigsaw of framed photos on the wall to her left. She floated a disinterested air into her voice. This was just a routine family errand. "Hello. I was hoping to get a copy of some family photographs my husband had developed here."

The man's eyes clouded as if he were measuring her words. Or her.

The lightness in her voice slipped. "I would like one copy of the set he picked up yesterday."

He tilted his head, his brow furrowing.

"Please?" She looked down at the name badge stuck to his white laboratory coat. "Simon?"

"Was there a problem with the photographs?" His voice was melodic and warm, marinated in honey.

"Not as such. We just need another—"

Simon's frown stopped her mid-sentence. "I can't do this for you."

"What do you mean you can't do this for me?"

"I sense you're not being honest with me."

"What does honesty have to do with it?"

Simon made his way around the counter. "Honesty has everything to do with it. I see this all the time—the world would be a better place if people owned up to what's going on in their lives. Don't you think so? Kelly?"

Kelly recoiled as if he'd slapped her across the face. "How do you know my name?"

With a light chuckle, Simon pointed to the Rubicon Pharma name badge on her suit jacket. "It looks like we're both branded." He guided her by the arm to the photo frames on the wall. "Let me show you what I mean about honesty."

Simon stopped in front of a large, black, wooden frame that held a close-up photo of a young woman's face. Behind her, a bathroom stall. Shame burned fierce in bloodshot eyes that looked beyond the camera.

Kelly peered at the photo, scouring for hidden meaning, and found none. "What's so honest about this?"

In silence, Simon moved along the wall. Photos of full wineglasses clutched behind backs. A suitcase thrown in the back of a taxi. A balding man in an unbuttoned business shirt slapped by a middle-aged woman in track pants and a San Francisco sweatshirt, a younger woman in a disheveled blouse clutching at his tie.

Whatever he was showing her, Kelly couldn't see it. "I'm sorry, but how is this honesty?"

Simon lightly traced a photo of a woman jamming cake into her mouth before tweaking the frame to straighten it. "These are the real images of these people, allowing us to see how they truly are. The camera never lies, you know."

A switch flicked in the deep recesses of Kelly's memory. She'd heard that before. And recently.

Simon moved past a photo of a man texting with one eye on his sleeping wife and stood in front of a large photograph in a thick, ornate golden frame. She saw an elevated bed next to a bank of machines, cords draping over the pillow, on which slept a young child. Red balloons floated above the pillow, wishing a speedy recovery. The child's mother, head in hands, leaned on an older man in animated discussion with a nurse.

Kelly gasped.

"I have seen this so many times. The first acknowledgment of truth—and the tightrope it presents."

Kelly's mind swirled, threatening to spin out of control. "What is this?"

"We all hide secrets. Sometimes they need to be revealed to nudge us in the direction we should take."

"This child could be hospitalized for any reason."

The warmth in Simon's voice carried the tinge of a harsh edge. "Really, Kelly?"

Kelly stared at the child in the hospital bed and then the mother's lowered head. Then she jumped as Simon rushed away from her and back to the counter. He reached below it for a thick, dog-eared notebook, a white-and-black-checkered pattern on the cover.

"I can't give you copies of the photos without the slip your husband would still have. It's a sacred contract I have with my customers. But if you can get that, it would be my pleasure to produce copies for you. On the spot, if you like."

But Kelly's eyes were glued to the child in the hospital. She couldn't make out the doctor's name on the sign above the child's bed, but it might as well have read Dr. Anthony Scott.

Twenty-One

The tiny bell above the door didn't jingle. With a slight tinkle and then a metallic crunch, it smashed against the freshly painted white of the doorframe as Daniel stormed into the film lab.

Simon stood behind the counter, his hands behind his back, that infuriating smile pasted across his face as he rose on the balls of his feet.

Daniel flung the envelope onto the counter. The photographs spilled and skidded across the glass top. "What do you call this?"

Simon looked down at them, a concerned sadness in his eyes. "I'm not sure what you mean." He picked up each photograph in white-gloved fingers and slipped them back into the envelope.

Daniel breathed hard and ragged, fueled by an anger that had percolated with every step from Crossroads. "You know exactly what I mean."

Simon removed one glove and lifted a last photo from the glass with a fingernail. A waft of sharp chemicals drifted from the processing unit behind him. The smell of something developing. He offered it to Daniel—the group photograph. "But these are the people behind your success."

Daniel's blood boiled in his ears. "Some things in these photographs didn't happen! Couldn't happen! It must have been you, using Photoshop in some kind of blackmail attempt. Who are you working with? Give me a name! Someone from another practice? Or is it my wife?"

Simon brushed off Daniel's anger like a bothersome fly, and then he leaned forward on splayed fingers. "The camera never lies, Daniel."

There was a pause in the universe, a moment in time as Daniel's subconscious stirred. The phrase from Gramps's camera again. The pounding in his chest checked itself, and he threw his head from side to side to shake off a growing dizziness. "Why do you keep saying that?"

Simon smiled as he made his way around the counter and then took Daniel by the elbow. He stood proudly to one side of the frames. "You see all these people here? They all came charging into my shop claiming things weren't as they seemed."

He waved a hand to the framed altercation between the balding, ruddy man and the woman in the San Francisco sweatshirt. "He told me the girl at work needed a mentor." A woman with cake falling from her mouth. "She was convincing everyone around her she was sticking to her diet." A man engrossed in whatever swept across his phone's screen while his wife slept next to him. "It was okay to watch some clips to spice up his marriage." A sick child in a hospital bed. "This child could be in the hospital for any reason."

Simon placed a hand on Daniel's shoulder, his breath warming his ear. "These are people who need to know truth, and they share something in common. They're hiding secrets that would be better out in the open where they could be dealt with. Surely you of all people would appreciate that?"

Daniel walked the length of the wall, now looking beyond the faces at the backgrounds. Telltale smoke curling from behind a back. Scrolling icons on a poker machine. Lipstick on a collar. White powder streaked on a face-up mirror. And an empty frame at the end of the row.

"How did you get these photographs?"

Simon pointed across the film lab. "They came from very special cameras."

Daniel noticed the gap in the lineup of cameras on the far wall. "What happened to the one with the bellows?"

A faraway look drifted across Simon's face. "The price was paid, and the camera is now telling its truth."

Daniel had played enough evasive games with people sitting on his couch to know when he needed to put down his foot—before his blood pressure got the better of the conversation. "So now you're telling me you sell magic cameras."

"The camera never lies. Never. You need to realize that. My cameras deliver the truth that needs to be delivered."

The lid to Daniel's self-control blew off. The veins in his neck pounded as his frustration escaped in an anguished scream, clenched fists shaking with rage. One held Gramps's camera.

Simon's face froze in an ecstatic grin. "The Olympus HS-10 Infinity. May I hold it?"

Daniel's anger seeped out of him at the same rate his brain was trying to make sense of what was going on.

"It's been so long since I've seen it. May I . . . please?"

So long since he'd seen it? Daniel's indignation kicked into gear in a vain attempt to maintain the rage.

Simon took Gramps's camera from Daniel's compliant hand with something approaching reverence. He wiped a gloved thumb across the viewfinder and appeared to be choking back tears. "This is such a special camera, Daniel."

Daniel had one final chance to put the conversation back on the rails. "I don't know what you're trying to achieve by pretending that the camera is somehow responsible—"

"It's as special as the day I sold it to your grandfather." Simon's eyes roved every inch of the camera.

White blotches fired in Daniel's vision. "What

166

did you say?"

Simon rose on the balls of his feet and beamed. "It's as special as it was the day I sold it to your grandfather . . . and he was right in choosing to give it to you."

Twenty-Two

The chatter in the Rubicon Pharma lecture theater dimmed with the lights. Murmurs rippled, driven by the morning's media naming of the drug responsible for the hospitalization of hundreds of young children. Mendacium was on page one but not for good reasons.

Kelly leaned across the armrest to Jasmine. "We'd better get some answers."

Jasmine shushed Kelly as smoke curled out from the black curtains at the back of the stage and colored lights ushered in pounding dance music. Tarquin Gascon paced out from the wings of the stage, and applause swept from one side of the auditorium to the other like wildfire. Rubicon Pharma welcomed its leader.

From her seat in the third row, Kelly stretched to hear any lulls in the applause, reassurance she wasn't alone in needing more than motivation and light shows.

Gascon stood center stage and lifted his arms like an Old Testament prophet. The crowd around Kelly rose as one in rapture as Gascon paced, his hands now clasped together in grateful thanks. "Thank you, everyone! My team! Thank you!"

Applause from the upper tiers fell around Kelly

like manna. When Jasmine glared at her, Kelly rose to her feet and mimed thunderous applause.

Gascon gestured for quiet, and seats were resumed.

Kelly raised her eyebrows at Jasmine. *Here goes.*

Gascon steepled his fingers under his nose as a perfect silence crept over the theater.

"You may have seen some unconfirmed—and scurrilous—media reports about side effects for a drug that might or might not be Mendacium. I will leave the damage control to our lawyers, but let's have a direct conversation about those rumors."

The crowd leaned into the truth Gascon was about to deliver.

"One, Mendacium has never been connected with any studies showing side effects in children. All of these media reports mention it, but where is the proof? What's that term? Fake news?"

Relieved laughter rippled around Kelly as she watched Gascon's careful tiptoeing through a prepared speech. A marionette operated by lawyers. "And two, we have never admitted liability for any issues with our products in the past."

The tiniest grunt escaped Kelly as she struggled to contain a cynical snigger. Even she knew that was what settlements were for.

Jasmine shot her a quick glance. Had that

snigger escaped? She glanced back at the stage and into the gaze of Gascon, who glared in her direction.

"So let's put these scurrilous rumors behind us. They're just a way for a jealous industry to try to bring us down. Now, moving on—"

Moving on? That was it? That was the proof Kelly was expected to deliver to doctors who cared about their patients?

"—to a great opportunity before us. Our research and development team has identified an emerging new disease of the twenty-first century that could benefit from our wonder drug, and sales will go through the roof!"

An excited chatter bounced around the lecture theater. Better sales meant one thing: bigger bonuses.

A screen rolled down from the ceiling above Gascon as the spotlights cut out. A young mother watched from her car as her children swung in slow motion on a playground, the sun shining through golden hair. "When I realized I had Restless Soul Syndrome, I thought my quality of life was over. But if there were a treatment I could take to give me purpose again, I'd be forever grateful . . ."

Kelly zoned out as the video rolled, swimming upstream against the enthralling current sweeping away everyone around her. This was the last straw. She could not look her clients in the face and sell a solution to this "syndrome" that hadn't existed five minutes ago.

Kelly scrolled her way through the news story on her desktop computer. Children were being hospitalized by the dozens because of side effects to medication. The main suspect? Mendacium. A spokesman for the company declined to comment. Kelly knew why.

She flicked a bittersweet glance to the family photos on her desk—the corporate reminder of a life being missed. She'd be able to spend more time with Milly if she quit her job—but leaving would carry a high price.

She jumped as her phone buzzed. Extension 664. Arnold. Kelly punched the screen. "Arnold, you're on speaker."

Arnold hesitated as if shelving a planned salvo. "My office." *Click.*

Kelly took a deep breath and one last, lingering look at her cubicle before heading past Jasmine toward the office at the end of the row. Jasmine raised her eyebrows with a mouthed *Good luck.*

With a polite knock, Kelly walked into a withering look of disapproval from her supervisor. He pointed to his empty guest chair.

Kelly sat, hands folded in her lap. Perhaps her choice would be made for her.

Arnold stared, his silence demanding a blurted apology from her.

Kelly's indignation rose. Why should she have to play games with this career middle manager? She wouldn't give him the pleasure. "I'm getting questions about the links between Mendacium and these side effects the media is reporting. And to meet the Rubicon Pharma 110 percent customer service guarantee, I need some answers."

Arnold sat bolt upright in his chair. "Links? What are they saying about links?"

A part of Kelly enjoyed watching the little man squirm. "I was looking forward to Mr. Gascon addressing that media attention like he promised, but I'm not sure he did—not in a way I can relay to my customers, anyway."

Arnold flushed beet red as his neck veins seemed to throb. "As our chief executive and leader, Mr. Gascon is not to be questioned. On anything. You are just looking to destabilize our team. That much was obvious when you interrupted our CEO in front of the entire company."

Kelly glanced around, horrified her snigger *had* escaped. "Arnold, I'm just trying to do the right thing. We're dealing with people's lives here. Children's lives."

Arnold oozed a greasy smile, leaned on his elbows, and drilled a gaze into Kelly. "No, we're in business. We have products. People have needs, and if they want our help, they will buy our product. That's how the marketplace works."

"But in our case, I want to make sure the marketplace doesn't make them sick—or worse."

The oil from Arnold's smile almost dripped down his chin. "While you're signing your career's death warrant, is there anything else?"

Kelly couldn't help herself. "So this Restless Soul Syndrome . . ."

Arnold rocked back in his chair. "Yes?"

"Seriously? How much research and development went into that?"

Arnold's smile broadened. "Are you suggesting we aren't thorough? A pharmaceutical company?"

Kelly bit her tongue before it gave her more cause for regret, but her silence answered for her.

"I see," Arnold said, sneering. "I'd love to fire you right here and now and march you from the premises myself, but Human Resources told me you need three warnings." He leaned forward on his elbows, which slipped on the edge of the desk, deflating his attempt at intimidation. "So consider this your first official warning."

Kelly stood. She had breathing room and time to work out how she would manage paying the price demanded of her.

Twenty-Three

D aniel's mouth flapped open like a goldfish on a sidewalk. Simon reached under the counter and pulled out a thick book with a black-and-white-checkered cover. He dropped it on the counter with a thud and thumbed through the dog-eared pages, his finger tracing line after line of transactions written in a block-like hand.

Simon knew Gramps?

"Now let's see . . . His was the Olympus HS-10 Infinity . . ." His finger stopped halfway down the page. "Here we are. Gordon Sumner. W.I.N. five dollars. Wow, that's coming up to ten years ago." Simon looked up at Daniel and smiled as he shook his head. "He took that long . . ."

Daniel's brain sputtered like the engine of an abandoned Chevy buried in a shed of junk. "How . . . What . . ."

Simon looked over Daniel's shoulder, a wistfulness dancing in his eyes. "It was a spring day, one of those days that make you want to quit your job and go on a perpetual picnic. You know the ones."

Whir, whir, whir. His thoughts still refused

to turn over. "Let me see that." He reached for the order book, but Simon swept it from the countertop.

"Gordon came in here a broken man. A pocket full of betting slips and eyes full of tears. He had only five dollars to his name."

Daniel's brain crawled out of the fog. "So he spent his last five dollars on a camera."

Simon patted the camera as it sat on the counter between them. "It's worth far more, Daniel, but he paid the price he needed to pay. He paid what was needed."

The tears sprang free at the memory of his beloved grandfather, spending the last of his money on what sounded like the one thing that saved him. Eventually.

Simon picked up the camera and brushed white-gloved fingers over the inscription with something approaching love. "He got it engraved like he said he would. He even went with the wording we discussed."

The wording they'd discussed? "But he never mentioned this camera shop before, and he would have at least dropped in to see me at my practice."

Simon smiled broadly at him. "I told you. This place is new, but I've had other camera shops. Anyway, he was a proud man, like you. Have you mentioned this place to your wife? Or your daughter?"

He hadn't. "How do you know about them?"

"They're in your photos. Your daughter is struggling at school, isn't she?"

Daniel blanched. His phone had only just pinged with the email. A formal warning from the school, driven by Mrs. Kowalick. Milly's grades weren't getting better. "How did you—"

"I've been having another conversation with someone about truth—"

"What truth?"

Simon held Gramps's camera up to his eye. "The camera is showing truth in your life . . . and in your family."

"Are you serious? A camera is showing truth? It makes more sense that you've been manipulating—"

"Well, can you explain some things? Like people appearing in your photos without you knowing?"

A single point had to elbow its way through a crowd of thoughts to get attention. "Easy to do in Photoshop, Simon. My twelve-year-old daughter could pull that off."

Simon wandered to a shelf in the back of the lab and selected a folder from a ceiling-high bookcase. He placed it on the counter and then flicked through pages of clear plastic sleeves, each holding strips of photographic negatives. He ran a white-gloved finger down a page until he reached the bottom row, pulling out a strip of negatives and holding it up to the light. "Number 24. Have a look for yourself."

Daniel held it up to the light as well. In the ghosted negative, reflections of his staff grouped on his deck, a person stood next to Peter with flowing black hair and thick white glasses. Howard.

"I'm not doctoring your photos, Daniel."

Daniel was unconvinced. "Double exposures, then?"

Simon laughed with a soft warmth. "That's often the next guess, but no. This is truth."

Looking closer at the negative, Daniel saw his black fingers entwined with Anna's. He shoved the strip toward Simon. "Truth, hey? This shows me cheating with Anna, and I'm not. I have done nothing wrong! If your magical camera shows truth, it got that one wrong."

"Perhaps the truth is in your heart. Others might not always see the truth people hold in their heart, but the camera never lies."

"I'm not buying it. It's possible that you just found out about Gramps. You didn't give me a chance to see the order book, so that could be a fake. There's no evidence you met Gramps, just a series of emotional hooks thrown into the water to catch me out. I've got to admit, you had me for a moment."

Simon threw a glance at the photos on the wall and rubbed his hands together. "That's okay.

Truth can be hard to accept the first time it's revealed."

"And stop talking like you're an inspirational bumper sticker."

The answer unfolded in front of him in frustrating simplicity. He'd buy some film and then test the camera on Kelly and Milly. If this camera was as special as Simon claimed, either he would find out what was happening with them or nothing would show up, giving him proof Simon was to blame. Fodder for the lawsuit to follow. Win-win.

He reached for his wallet. "I think I will buy some film from you this time."

Twenty-Four

The gravel in his driveway crunched under Daniel's feet as he strode to his front door. Cameras that took their own photos? He scoffed under his breath. Forty-four dollars to get his photos was cheap if it provided answers to either Kelly and Milly's problems or the opening statement in a lawsuit against Simon.

"Kelly? Milly?"

An unexpected echo from Daniel's footsteps rang throughout the house, pricking the growing bubble of indignation that had built on the drive home. He raced up the stairs before lightly tapping on his daughter's bedroom door. "Mill?"

Nothing.

A harder rap. "Milly?"

Still nothing. He pushed on the door and stood on the threshold of invading his daughter's privacy. As he eased his way into Milly's sanctuary, the guilt kicked into gear but was dissipated by the image of his princess teetering on the handrail of their deck. The image that appeared in Daniel's vision every time he blinked. The last thought that crawled into his head as he dropped off to sleep and ambushed him at first light.

He had to know.

Her bedroom was immaculate. Social commentators who preached every teenager lived in a foot-deep squalid pile of discarded food and clothing had never met his daughter. Her creaseless quilt, cushions casually thrown but strategically placed. Pencils at ninety degrees in perfect alignment. Her laptop on her desk, a single photograph bouncing around the screen while it dozed. An eight-year-old Milly, her arms hooked around her parents' shoulders, the glue in a happy family embrace.

Daniel woke the laptop with a tap and was confronted with a password window. He raised a finger but then stopped. The answers to Milly's problems might lie behind that lock, but hacking into his daughter's computer was a level of invasion he couldn't stomach.

Her phone nestled in its charger, its only other home outside of her hand. It sat in the shadow of a happy family memory—a framed portrait. Daniel picked up Milly's phone, and the sense of intrusion again pushed down on him.

Another flash of Milly on the railing. He had to know.

Daniel woke her phone. No password. He stepped into his daughter's world and scrolled through her messages. Nothing save for midafternoon pleas for rides home or messages to one parent demanding the location of the other.

Only two names appeared in her message list—his and Kelly's. His brow furrowed. Where were the messages from her friends? They had to be chatting elsewhere.

Daniel hunted for social media. Their conversations about the dangers of social media seemed to have worked; she had nothing installed. No strange phone numbers. No Google searches to raise concerns. Milly's phone was proving as much a closed book as she was.

He had one last place to check. Her photos. He thumbed through them, stunned at what he found.

Milly didn't appear in any of them. Neither did anyone at school.

A constant loop of photos featuring her parents crushed his expectation of an endless roll of selfies. Every photo showed him and Kelly together. His thumb scrolled through her memories. Even when they were in the same room but not in the same conversation, Milly found a way to take a photo of them together, and then she linked them with overlaid hot-pink love hearts or smiling emojis.

Daniel's thumb skidded to a halt. The altercation with Monique was also featured on Milly's phone, but she had cropped out Monique. Kelly, frozen mid-sentence in a moment of attack, was now talking to Daniel.

Daniel sank onto the end of Milly's bed. What type of kid took a hundred photos, none of them featuring herself? What type of kid never shared them? Did she lie in bed at night flicking through photos that showed her family happy? Was there something more to her than failing grades? The lack of evidence that she was a normal kid waved a red flag.

Downstairs the front door slammed, and Daniel dropped the phone. The one thing worse than snooping in Milly's room was being caught snooping in Milly's room. Daniel leaped to his feet, plugged in the phone, and then placed it next to her family photo, a time of genuine smiles. He had to find a way back there again.

As he closed Milly's door silently behind him, he still had no answers. The price for breaching his daughter's trust would be high, but the return was nothing. All he had left now was the camera.

Daniel laughed as he realized the insanity of that thought. Daniel Whiteley, with a master's in counseling, bestselling author and counselor to thousands, now placed his trust in a magical camera?

Daniel again lifted the camera to his eye. "This time, how about Milly and Nan?"

His mother reached for her granddaughter, who scowled as Daniel peered through the viewfinder. "Smile, Milly!" She pasted on a fake smile that would have been at home on the couch in his office.

He squeezed the trigger with a satisfying *clunk*. "Now a photo of all three of you?"

Kelly stepped into the frame, and Daniel squinted through the viewfinder, analyzing all three expressions for clues. His mother smiled broadly, Milly frowned, and Kelly looked past the camera and over his shoulder.

"Let's at least try to look like a happy family!"

His mother's smile grew, Milly's frown etched deeper, and Kelly continued to look over his shoulder, a disinterested boredom building the longer he took. Daniel snuck a look with his free eye. Kelly now smiled at the camera.

Another satisfying *clunk*. There were no surprises here. This was looking more like a lawsuit every minute.

His mother shuffled toward him. "I have no recent photos of you three!"

Daniel's grip on the camera tightened as he reached into his pocket. "Take one with my phone, and then I can email it to you."

Three quizzical faces peered at him, and Kelly spoke for them all. "What's wrong with the camera you're holding?"

Warmth from the embarrassment of the knee-jerk reaction that had revealed a little too much crept up his neck. He had no idea why he'd done that. He tried to laugh off their suspicion. "Um, sure."

Daniel handed the camera to his mother and then stood next to Milly.

His mother became flustered as she held her father's camera. Tears welled behind her thick glasses. "This is the first time I've held this . . ." She wiped away the tears and pushed her glasses to her forehead. "Big smiles, everyone!"

Daniel grinned at the camera before flicking a glance at his daughter. She was smiling. At last.

His mother lowered the camera. "Lovely. When will I get to see these?"

"I'll be at the film lab later today, so probably tomorrow." Or never, depending on what Simon did with the film.

"I'll drop you home, Charlotte." Kelly reached for her handbag.

Daniel kissed his mother's cheek in a good-bye and then stood in the foyer as the two women headed for Kelly's car.

He turned to the kitchen, intent in his step. He had to know, and now he had a chance to find out.

"Hey, Mill, why don't we have some ice cream?"

He moved to the kitchen as Milly made her wary way onto a tall wicker chair.

Daniel strode to the freezer under the guarded gaze of his daughter. "It's been a while since we've talked."

"Not a lot of talking goes on here at all, Dad." She met his gaze.

He passed her a bowl filled way past Kelly's usual limit of an appropriate amount of ice cream. "How about we trade questions. I'll ask one, you ask one."

"Okay."

"What are you worried about most at the moment?"

Milly scooped ice cream into her mouth. "I'm worried you and Mom will break up."

"What makes you think we might?"

Milly shushed him with a held-up spoon. "My turn. Why don't you and Mom talk anymore?"

Daniel thought for a moment. "That's normal for couples who've been married for some time. They end up so busy that they spend all of their time together just trying to make things work."

Milly studied him over her bowl.

"Or they stop listening to each other's needs and expect that their partner thinks about life the same way they do."

Daniel took in another mouthful of ice cream. Now that one question was out of the way, this was the time to find out. "Okay, my turn. Why did you stand on the railing during the work dinner the other night?"

On her face, a flash of thunder clashed with her innocence.

"Someone saw you, Milly."

She flushed. "But I didn't." The frail bond fostered by the first few spoonfuls of ice cream cracked.

"Come on, Mill. If you want honesty, you need to be honest yourself."

Milly glared at him. "I *am* being honest. I didn't do that even if I was thinking about it."

Daniel studied her. The crinkling around her eyes. The twitch of a lip. She *was* being honest. So Simon had doctored that photograph too.

"That's okay, Mill. I believe you. I'm sorry."

But how did Simon know she was thinking about standing on the railing?

The gravel crunched in the driveway. Why was Kelly back so quickly? Daniel couldn't push things too far. Anyway, if this camera was all Simon said it was, he'd have his answers tomorrow. "You know, it's okay to talk about it with us. Let's have no secrets, okay?"

"Dad, I've got one last question."

Kelly's keys jingled in the front door.

"I don't know how to say it."

"That's okay. Let me have it." He smiled as he scraped the last of his ice cream from his bowl.

Milly stared at her spoon as it made its slow way around the rim of her bowl. "What do you think of Anna?"

Kelly burst through the front door and beelined for the kitchen counter. "Forgot my phone." She

186

took one disapproving look at the bowls of ice cream and bustled back out the door.

Daniel waited for the departing crunch of tires on gravel. "She's been a good friend over the years, she helped me build the business, and she's a great counselor. In fact, she told me you two connected at the dinner, and she's offered to talk further with you." This was good. Milly was leading the conversation in his preferred direction.

But her face clouded over, her brows knotted.

"I'm glad you mentioned Anna, but why did you ask me what I think of her?"

Her spoon froze, and a look of terror flashed into her eyes. "Because when I took the photo of everyone else on the deck, it looked like you were holding hands with her."

Twenty-Five

Kelly stood frozen to the spot outside the laundromat, the words from her phone ringing in her ears.

"Say that again?"

Dr. Scott's voice hardened, and the gravity of his repeated point landed hard. "Two of my patients are in the hospital because of a reaction to Mendacium, and I need to know what's going on."

Kelly's world whirled. Children were sick, and she was to blame. She could have warned Anthony, but she hadn't for one simple reason: to save her own situation. She stared at the hand-painted cardboard sign in the window: "Coming clean! Laundromat now open!!!"

If only it were that easy.

"Anthony, I'll call you back in a few minutes." She needed to think.

A battle raged within her. On one side were sick children. On the other side lay honesty without a home in which to live. Between them the company line Rubicon Pharma expected her to toe. Either way, children would suffer—Dr. Scott's patients or her own daughter. Simon was right about the tightrope. The sense of vertigo was paralyzing.

The little bell jingled as Kelly pushed on the door to Simon's Film Lab.

Simon turned from straightening photo frames. "Wonderful to see you again, Kelly. How can I help you today?"

Kelly had been rehearsing her line since she dropped off Charlotte. "I know you told me you couldn't give me a copy of Daniel's photos, but he told me there were problems with them. I need to know what those problems are."

Simon leaned back on the frames and frowned. "Is Daniel having problems with his photos?"

"He says that's why he can't show them to me."

Simon dropped his head. "Well, if that's what he says, then he's having problems with his photos." He moved past her to the counter.

Kelly's words tumbled out, her well-crafted argument fracturing with Simon's casual dismissal. "I was hoping you could give me a copy of his photos so I can find out what's going on with him."

"I'm afraid I can't. We have a sacred contract, but I am pleased you've been honest with me."

"Why can't I get his photos? I'm his wife, and I need to know what's going on." She threw a frustrated look at the frames on the wall. One of them had changed. The balding man in the unbuttoned business shirt and the middle-aged woman in track pants and a San Francisco sweatshirt were no longer fighting. Now they were smiling, an arm around each other, the orange of the sweatshirt now a pale beige.

Simon studied her. "You look troubled."

Kelly snapped a look back at him. "Of course I'm troubled. My biggest concern right now is that I can't get copies of Daniel's photos."

Simon smiled. "Is it?"

"I'm also dealing with an issue at work—"

"Side effects and sick children?"

"How do you know?"

Simon nodded to her name tag and then leaned against the counter, his voice mellowing in a singsong cadence. "I've been following the news, you know. Tell me about it."

Her emotions bubbled up and the shaky wall she had built to hold them back crumbled. The excuses she was supposed to peddle. Made-up syndromes that didn't need medical help. And now children sick from medication she was pushing. "My integrity keeps running into my company's profitability."

Simon gestured to the wall of frames. "I hear that a lot. And I've found over the years that the opposite of profit isn't loss. The opposite of profit is people."

Kelly regained her breath, enthralled by his advice. Warmed by his voice.

"You're not alone, Kelly. It's one of the downsides of our modern world, like when you hear the gambling authority give a rapid-fire warning about responsible gambling after a thirty-second tease about a life-changing lottery ticket. Or the beer manufacturer's casual advice to drink responsibly after preaching how popular you will be when you don't. Or in your case, promising the world to people and then telling them it's their fault for listening to you."

"I can't be a part of this anymore. What do I do?"

"Now that you're convicted of the truth in your life, you need to be honest about it."

"But I'll lose the house."

Simon lifted a finger and wandered to the wall, stopping in front of the thick, ornate gold frame. "You'll lose a lot more if you don't."

"Everyone lies, Simon."

Simon stared at the photo in silence.

Kelly moved toward it. There was the slightest movement—like the flitter of hummingbird wings—and her breath drifted away. Now she saw two sick children in the hospital, wired into monitors crowding their tiny beds. And the name above the beds was crystal clear in thick, black pen: Dr. Anthony Scott.

Time slowed as the photo drifted in and out of her focus. "Who are you?"

A tear formed in the corner of Simon's eye. "I am a seeker of truth. I help others seek it too."

Kelly's glance flickered back to the frame. This was inescapable truth.

"Truth isn't easy, Kelly. Everyone holds secrets. But most often life is better without them."

The waft of chemicals reached Kelly's nose. The smell of something developing.

Simon raised a finger to the second child in a hospital bed, her wide, sad eyes begging for relief. "Why don't we start here? What if that were Milly?"

Simon had taken a metaphorical ax to the barrier her conscience had built. As it splintered into a thousand pieces, Kelly knew what she had to do next. Her hand crept to her pocket and pulled out her phone. In slow motion, she punched in a number that had haunted her for days.

The tears trickled down Simon's cheeks.

"Dr. Scott's rooms, please." Then, "Alisha, it's Kelly Whiteley from Rubicon. I need to speak to Anthony. It's urgent."

"I'm sorry, but he's unavailable at the moment."

A slow smile lit up Simon's face.

"This is urgent, Alisha. He's waiting for my call."

A pause. "One moment."

"Thanks for getting back, Kelly." Anthony's warm tone was back.

Kelly cut a swath through the pleasantries. "Anthony, you asked me about the potential side effects of Mendacium. I have no data to back this up, but I know we can't rule them out.

I can't guarantee anything, and I understand your nervousness at not having that guarantee. I suggest if you're concerned, you contact our R&D department for any information to help you make the best decision for your patients."

A pause. "Are you saying what I think you're saying? What you're able to say?"

"Yes, I am. It's something I need to say." The phone trembled in her hand.

"You have great integrity."

"Thank you." Kelly's voice eked out of her in a whisper. With shaking fingers, she cut the call. The growing sense of dread that eased into her was met with a warmth. A peace. A feeling of right that calmed her quivering nerves.

Tears cascaded down Simon's face. "I am so proud of you. Now, how would you like to save more than just one family?"

Twenty-Six

Daniel stood just inside his mother's front door and wished she could stay on the point. He needed to arm himself with as much information about Gramps's camera as possible before he picked up his photos and confronted Simon.

"How are you and Kelly?"

"We have our moments, but we're busy people. A lot of families are like us right now. It's the modern world."

"You were always good at turning things into an academic argument, and you didn't answer my question."

"Of course we're doing well. Work's great. Just had our thousandth couple."

His mother smiled. "You've worked so hard, and everything was set up by your wonderful book." A shiver ran up Daniel's spine. "And you still didn't answer my question."

"We're having some trouble, but we'll work through it."

His mother reached up to stroke his cheek. "Thank you. I'm glad, because I'm worried about Milly. She looks like you did at twelve, just before your father left. You withdrew into yourself and kept asking how your dad could love another woman."

Daniel winced at the sting from the memory. He became a marriage counselor to stop anyone else from feeling the pain he had when his family home fell quiet one night and stayed quiet. Then a chill washed over him as Milly's innocent accusation raised its head. She couldn't have seen him holding Anna's hand that night, because he hadn't. She must have seen the photo, but how? And what else had she seen?

His mother wasn't finished. "And I'm really concerned about her schooling, Daniel. I've asked her a few times now about her school report, and she keeps avoiding the question. She has always been such a good student. What about her scholarship? Won't that put extra pressure on your finances?"

Daniel absorbed the barrage of questions from his mother with a sense of annoyed urgency. He needed to get her back on track. "I think by tomorrow I'll have some answers to what's bugging Milly. Anyway, I need to know more about Gramps's camera."

His mother folded her hands. "Something has been bothering me since you mentioned it. Who would take a photo of him with a betting slip?"

"I don't know. Probably Garth."

"So why wouldn't Garth tell me?"

"Sometimes coming to terms with things is the

hardest part of being honest with people. Maybe he didn't want us to think badly of Gramps. So, back to the camera—when did he get it?"

"Ten years ago, maybe? When he first got it he took photos of everyone around him but showed them to no one. He was so possessive of it but so generous with everything else."

"Do you know where he got it?"

"No, I don't."

Daniel deflated. Another dead end.

His mother clicked her fingers. "Although if you asked Garth, he would almost certainly know."

Daniel strode up the well-kept path that wound its way to the neat ground-floor apartment. He breathed in the smell of fresh paint on the front door and the perfume wafting from large pots filled with flashes of color. Then he glanced down at a mat that welcomed friends to this home. The photographs in Gramps's photo album flashed back to him. Garth, slumped in the doorway in a back alley, broken teeth jagging at all angles below a beanie jammed down over wispy white hair. Homeless.

He had just ten minutes until his photos would be ready.

The front door opened to a beaming grin of pearly white teeth above a crisp, white linen shirt and a full head of white hair slicked to one side.

Well, that answered that. That photo must have been Garth's time volunteering in some kind of homeless program.

"Come in, come in, boy!" Garth ushered Daniel into a hallway with a floor rug that ran in perfect symmetry down the middle of polished floorboards. Daniel followed Garth into a small kitchen with a laminated table and two vinyl chairs pushed up against the far wall.

Garth strode to the stove. "Would you care for coffee?"

"I can't stay, Garth, but—"

Garth pulled out two coffee mugs. "It's a little lonely without my regular bridge partner, but when you get to this age, saying good-bye to your friends is just a normal part of life."

"We all miss him terribly."

Garth placed a steaming mug in front of Daniel. "There's not much left of him apart from memories . . . or photos."

The perfect opportunity. "That's what I wanted to talk to you about. He left me his camera." He left the sentence hanging to see if any expression developed. It didn't.

"He went everywhere with that camera. Mind you, he let nobody use it. I picked it up one day, and he got very angry."

Daniel felt the sinking disappointment of another approaching dead end. "I'm trying to find out more about why it was a special camera."

Again he left the sentence hanging like a fishhook. Garth didn't rise to the bait.

"I'm so pleased you came to visit. I rarely have people in my home."

That final word echoed in Daniel's head. Home. "How long have you lived here?"

"Thirty years. Joan passed ten years ago next month."

Thirty years. That was it, then. He'd never lived on the streets.

Garth's eyes glazed over as he fell into a river of nostalgia. "One thing about your Gramps is that the older he got, the clearer his vision became. He could see through you like you were made of glass. You couldn't hide anything from him."

Daniel built up enough silence for Garth to fill the space with information. It worked.

"I'm glad he could. I had a drinking problem, you know. At first it was to cope with losing Joan, and I had a glass of wine to manage the loneliest of nights. But then it became a way for me to manage the toughest of days. Then just any day. I didn't realize how much it was managing me."

Daniel took a deep mouthful of too-hot coffee and choked as he swallowed the burning liquid. He had to move Garth along.

"I was hiding my drinking from everyone. No one knew, or so I thought. Then one day your

Gramps sat me down—in that very chair you're sitting in—and told me he could see my heart and how I would end up if I kept drinking."

See my heart . . . Another forced gulp of burning coffee.

"Gordon told me if I kept going, I would end up on the street, lonely and alone. Sleeping in back alleys in the cold, leaning against doors. And he told me he wouldn't be able to live with himself if he could see me heading down that path and did nothing about it. Thank goodness I listened."

Daniel stared into his coffee mug as time slowed.

The photos couldn't be real. They couldn't show the truth.

Garth looked around his little kitchen. "I could have lost everything, but he stepped in. To this day I have no idea how he knew."

But Daniel did. He just couldn't believe it.

Twenty-Seven

The rhythmic tapping of Kelly's fingernails on the meeting table drew a raised eyebrow from Jasmine. "You look different. Patch things up with Daniel?"

Kelly held her breath as, from the doorway, Arnold surveyed the seats for their team meeting. He took the one closest to the door, and Kelly breathed again. The unoccupied chair next to her stayed unoccupied. "No, but I am working my way through a few things."

Arnold clapped for the attention of a team glued to their cell phones. "People, we're just waiting for the new addition to our team . . . Here she is now."

A young woman, blond tresses flowing over her salmon-pink suit jacket and crisp white blouse, surveyed the room for a seat. The blonde from the stage who looked like Monique. She excused her way into the room and headed directly for Kelly, who moved her chair over a bit, not to give her newest colleague space, but herself. Even up close, this young woman was impossible perfection, all angles and curves in the right places.

Jasmine elbowed her as she reached a

welcoming hand across to their newest team member.

Arnold called back their attention. "Tiffany will join us in a new role of serving the clinics in the west of our city."

Tiffany flashed a flawless smile around the room, and Kelly aged twenty years in an instant. Then the impact of Arnold's statement arrived in a rush. The clinics in the west belonged to her.

Arnold thumbed through his iPad. "The CEO has asked all team leaders to read through this memo. It would appear that one of our city's clinics has called R&D about these scurilous"—he glared at the team around the table—"and untrue rumors about Mendacium." He scanned his team, searching for telltale signs.

An icy rush whipped through Kelly as Arnold offered an oily smile to her end of the table. Then relief. The angle was wrong, thankfully. The smile was for Tiffany.

"It also appears they were advised to do this by one of our sales representatives, and while they didn't mention which one, we are launching an internal investigation to find out." He again scanned the team, licking his lips with anticipation. Another smile dripped toward her end of the room.

Kelly's leg jackhammered under the table. She fought hard to stop it from powering her chair through the ceiling.

Arnold resumed his narration. "Rubicon Pharma is a team. A family. We're all working toward the same goals, so we cannot tolerate this dissension." His eyes swept the room as he apparently drew from his memorization of this part, his voice rising as if relishing the message he was delivering. "We will hold an official inquiry to find the guilty party and get to the bottom of what, we presume, is just a misunderstanding."

He sent another oily smile toward Kelly's end of the table, but this time it was directed at her.

Kelly stared at her desktop, frozen in fury and terror.

Jasmine leaned back from the divider between them. "I wouldn't want to be in that rep's shoes."

Kelly was lost in her stare, her brain abandoning any attempt at thought.

"Oh, Kel, it's not you, is it?"

A single nod.

"But you're already on one warning."

"I know."

"You couldn't help yourself, could you?"

"Children are sick, Jasmine, because of something I sell. That's not right."

Jasmine's eyes darted around the cubicles in their corporate prairie. "You had better keep your voice down."

Kelly knew what she had to do. It was time to save more than the one family whose children appeared on Simon's wall. She stood and smoothed her jacket. "Now is the time for my voice to be heard. I'm going to talk to Arnold."

"What, throw yourself on the mercy of the court?"

"No, it's just the right thing to do." Kelly walked past an openmouthed Jasmine to the office at the end of the row. She took a deep breath and knocked.

Arnold's smile oiled up at the sight of her. "I'm writing an email to you."

Kelly took a seat on the edge of his guest chair.

Arnold leaned back and laced his arms behind his head. "I've heard back from R&D, and I know which clinic called—"

"It's one of mine."

Arnold frowned. She had taken the wind out of his sails. Good.

Kelly held her head high. "I can give you the exact wording of our conversation, if you like. The doctor had two children reporting symptoms similar to the side effects we're trying to pretend don't exist, and I told him if he wanted information, he could get it from our R&D team. If these rumors are as untrue as we keep claiming them to be, then what's the problem with proving it?"

Arnold's mouth flopped open as Kelly pressed her finger into his desk.

"I've read my contract and the Human

Resources manual, and nothing in there says my behavior or the wording of my conversation is a sackable offense. A formal warning at worst, but not sackable. In fact, if anything, I have fulfilled the obligations of our customer service guarantee."

Arnold deflated, his attack robbed of fuel. He tried to sit tall in his chair and resume his self-appointed role of executioner. "It's not your role to determine what punishment fits the crime. Until we can speak to this doctor, I'm giving you your second formal warning—"

Kelly stood tall, flooded with righteous intent. "Actually, save it. I quit."

"You don't get to quit—" But Kelly was already out the door.

One half of her was lifting her integrity shoulder high and celebrating a win. The other half of her was picturing how much work it would take to sell her car or, heaven forbid, the house.

And how she'd tell Daniel.

Twenty-Eight

Daniel sauntered toward Simon's counter, behind which lay the answers he needed. He had examined every option, and each one was a winner. If these photos showed him "truth" about Milly and Kelly, he would confront them with it. But if they denied it, he would sue Simon for doctoring the photos. Last, if there was nothing wrong with them, then Simon had at least Photoshopped his first photos, and he would still sue him—for everything he had. He wouldn't even need the money from a second book.

These photos had to be nothing. Garth had just unnerved him.

The thin strap of the camera cut into his shoulder. He had to keep it nearby at least until he could prove how this was happening.

Simon rose on the balls of his feet, an envelope on the counter in front of him, its proud sticker sealing the evidence Daniel wanted. No, needed.

Daniel lay his work folder, a copy of *No Secrets*, and Gramps's camera on the counter. "Good morning, Simon!"

Simon beamed. "You look like you're in a good mood."

"I'm about to have a great day. Either I find out

what Milly and Kelly won't tell me or I've got ammunition for my lawyers to take you to the cleaners."

Simon chuckled. "That's the right approach, if you will accept truth." He held out the envelope for Daniel to take. Daniel took hold of it, but Simon didn't let go.

Daniel snatched it from him and ripped it open. Daniel frowned. "Just three photos? I took more than that. And how can you get away with charging me forty-four dollars for three photos?"

Simon rose on the balls of his feet. "Three is all you need."

The first photo showed a frowning Milly with his mother, smiling in that awkward way of hers. That was nothing new.

He flicked to the second photo, which showed all three women in his life. Again, his mother smiled, an arm around Milly. Milly again frowned, and Kelly looked over Daniel's shoulder as if waiting for someone to enter the room. The same look he'd seen through the viewfinder.

Daniel dropped the photos onto the counter and looked up at Simon with a flash of triumph. "No surprises at all here. Lawyer up, buddy."

Pure ecstasy flooded through Simon's face. "All three photos?"

Daniel picked up the envelope and flicked to the final picture. He stood in his own kitchen, an arm around his daughter, who this time was smiling. But the person to Milly's right wasn't Kelly.

It was Anna.

Daniel threw the photo into Simon's face. "Right. That's it! I will sue you for everything you've got."

Simon clasped his hands behind his back. "The camera never lies, Daniel. It's showing truth in your life."

Daniel scoffed. "Truth? All I see is evidence of you manipulating my photos. You will hear from my lawyer when I inform him of your extortion attempt."

Simon's face hardened as his voice carried a flint edge. "Extortion? Over what? Showing that your heart is drifting to another and away from your wife? That your daughter is unhappy?" Simon spread his fingers on the counter. "And are you sure you want anyone else to know why the front cover of *No Secrets* sometimes doesn't have your name on it?"

Daniel's mouth slid open.

"Truth cannot simply be avoided, covered up, or ignored, and the camera chooses the truth it shows."

Daniel found his voice—just. "The camera chooses the truth it shows?"

"Yes, like when people are unhappy but hide behind a smile. Or when they pretend to be someone they're not to impress people they don't like anyway."

Daniel felt his face redden. "So you've read my book, then?"

Simon nodded at the copy of *No Secrets*. "*Your* book?"

Daniel flushed, feeling an overwhelming urge to punch this Simon guy square in the mouth. But throwing an assault charge on top of everything else was the last thing he needed.

"Yes, my book." He checked himself. "Well, *our* book."

Simon sized him up. "I don't create the truth that's there, but I certainly help breathe it into life. If you still think I've manipulated your photos, let me prove my innocence."

He grabbed Gramps's camera from the counter and then marched to the shelves and reached down for a roll of film. He loaded it into the back of the camera and held it out to Daniel. Then he picked up *No Secrets* and clasped it to his lab coat with the front cover in full view.

"Take a photo of your book." He checked himself. "*Our* book."

"Why?"

Simon's hands shook as his voice tremored with anger. "You want proof of the camera's power? Take a photo of the book, and if it still says you wrote it, then sue me."

Daniel held the camera up to his eye and the

lens twitched into focus. It couldn't be. He lowered his hands.

The book still trembled in Simon's hand, but there was flint in his voice. "Is there a problem?"

Daniel again looked through the viewfinder. His name was erased from *No Secrets*. He lowered the camera, his head spinning with secrets, cameras, books, and photos. "But how did Anna get into my photos?"

Simon's voice softened. Warmed. "The camera is revealing the truth in your heart."

"But I have done nothing wrong!"

"What would you say if you heard that from a man sitting on the couch in your office?"

Daniel stood admonished. He knew what he would say. He'd tell the guy if he'd already left emotionally, he might as well have left physically.

"You are seeing where your heart is."

The words from Gramps's letter. The film lab spun in Daniel's vision.

"Who are you?"

Simon splayed his fingers on the counter as a fresh waft of chemicals hit Daniel. "I am a seeker of truth. I thought you were too."

The decisions of the past swirled around him. He was under pressure with a fledgling counseling practice on the financial rocks, taking his career with it. Howard's manuscript was just there, and Howard wasn't.

Simon nodded knowingly. "There's always a reason, but that doesn't turn a lie into truth."

Daniel blinked hard. "So now you can read my mind?"

A grin crept across Simon's features. "No, your face. And you're thinking you had a good reason for doing what you did. At the time, you probably did, but the consequences of today don't always respect the actions of yesterday."

Daniel couldn't let this get out. If it did, his career would be over, and there was no way Kelly would accept that the photo on the deck, him holding hands with Anna, wasn't real. He'd lose his career and his family. It all carried a high price.

Simon leaned across the counter to Daniel, his voice quiet. Sympathetic. Almost like a counselor. "The price will be higher if you don't. The camera never lies, Daniel. You can try to hide from it, but I think it would be better if you dealt with your secrets, brought them out into the open and faced them."

The knots in Daniel's jaw flexed. "I'll take care of it."

"How has that worked for you so far?"

An escape hatch opened in his mind, a solution tinged with sadness. He just had to get rid of the camera, Gramps's last gift to him.

Simon's whisper floated across the counter with the whiff of chemicals. "If you're thinking it would be easier to get rid of the camera rather than face your secrets, I would advise against it."

But Daniel already knew this was the only door open to him.

Twenty-Nine

Daniel rested his chin on his arms as the camera stared him down from across his home desk, unblinking. He had to take control, in his own way. In his own time. He didn't want to get rid of it—Gramps's last gift—but it also couldn't stay.

His plan unfolded like an origami tutorial. Lock the camera in Gramps's briefcase, behind a combination known to him alone. Then he would sit in his office chair until inspiration for his second book came. He would confront Kelly and get her stuff out into the open, take Milly to see Anna, and put in more effort at home. Everyone at work would need to know the group photo didn't work, and he would email Monique, clarifying their professional relationship in writing. Her recent absence had given him some much-needed breathing space anyway.

Daniel threw open the door to his closet and stared at the briefcase on the floor. Not that long ago the dusty leather and burnished silver were a treasured gift. He opened the clasps with a *thunk*. A wave of sadness washed over him, carried on a tide of drifting Old Spice.

Daniel turned the camera over in his hands,

still unable to comprehend the events of the past few days. A camera that revealed truth? It hadn't revealed truth about Kelly or Milly in those other two photos.

He reached into the briefcase and pulled out the faded red album, and then he flicked through the pages, scanning for truth. He examined the photos of Gramps's friends. Fingers splayed in front of a computer screen; though out of focus, enough flesh showed between them to suggest the type of website being visited. A curl of cigarette smoke winding its way out from behind an older woman as she watched her grandchildren from a doorway.

Then a thought. Could the camera work in counseling? A few snaps, and he could sift the lies from the truth. That would build his reputation in a big hurry, and he wouldn't need a second book *or* a lawsuit.

The cardboard groaned as Daniel reached Garth's photo. He was never on the streets even though Gramps had warned him he could be. He stared hard at Garth's broken teeth. The photo looked so real, but why was the color so washed out? Gramps's photo was next. Daniel spun in his chair to see Gramps's recliner. Why was it a dull pink in this photo?

With another stiff groan of the pages, the state of his marriage appeared in vivid color. Daniel turned away from Kelly, staring off into the distance. That could easily be true. The next page, his smile at someone off camera. Another page, Milly crying at the party. While he hadn't been able to find out if that was true, it might as well have been.

He slapped the album shut. He was over-thinking. This had to end.

He placed the camera in the briefcase. Then he reached into his shirt pocket and threw the film slip from Simon's Film Lab on top of the camera. His thumbs whirred the combination out of sync, and Gramps's briefcase resumed its place hidden away from the world. He leaned back on the closed door, the threat neutralized, his secret now safe and back under his control. He would reveal it when he was ready.

The screen saver on his laptop flashed the front cover of *No Secrets*. He thumped the space bar, more to banish the image than to wake his computer. A document appeared on screen. Ten pages of words extracted by nervous sweat and teeth-grinding anxiety. Few worth reading. None worth publishing.

His chair bounced as he sat with intent, and Daniel took a deep breath, fuel for his inspiration. He would force this book out whether it liked it or not.

It didn't like it.

Several halting sentences tiptoed their way onto his screen as if scared to wake the delete key. Daniel grimaced as he typed, the words in his head not willing to sentence themselves to a short-lived existence. Daniel dropped his head, and with a mighty roar, he pounded his fists on the desk.

The echo of his anger dissipated as a soft knock sounded at the door. It edged open to reveal Kelly.

She bit her lip, and tears sprang forth. Daniel jumped up and hurried forward as her emotions spilled out in a gush. "I quit today . . . One doctor asked me about side effects . . . I couldn't lie if it will hurt children . . . He called Rubicon himself."

Daniel placed his hands on her jerking shoulders. "You quit your job?"

The sobs bubbled from her. "Somebody told Arnold . . . playing his usual power games . . . told me to toe the company line, so I told him to shove it."

Daniel embraced her. "Wow."

Kelly sobbed as he stroked her hair. "If you thought you were endangering others, you did the right thing."

"I know what it means in terms of the house. We'll just have to tide things over until this book is finished."

Daniel lost the battle with his rising defensiveness, and his shutters slid up. Kelly stood back and looked up at him as she gulped down her sobs. "Why is it taking so long?"

The last of Daniel's resolve cracked. He had to tell her. "I can't just come up with another book. I've appreciated your patience up to this point, and I need you to hang in there for a little longer until I can deliver it."

"But you did last time . . . and it happened so fast. I don't understand."

The cold blade of her challenge sliced deep into his anxiety, and any answers flitted back into the shadows.

Kelly took another step back. "You can't tell me much nowadays. What about those photos you took of us? Why were you so intent on taking them?" His silence lit the fuse of Kelly's frustration. "Why can't you talk to me? Daniel, we need to talk to someone. This has reached the point where I can't stay if things will be like this."

Her threat hung heavy in the air, and it fueled a growing anger. With everything he was dealing with, now she played that card? "I'm a marriage counselor with a bestselling book about marriage. It's not as simple as me seeing a marriage counselor."

Kelly's lips pursed below hard eyes and tear-streaked cheeks. "So you're choosing your reputation over me? Unless there are other reasons you don't want to see someone."

Daniel's voice rose in defense. "Are we back here again? You aren't in a position to talk about refusing to see someone. I've already suggested we talk to Anna, but you won't."

"Ah yes, your work-wife. Can't you see why I don't want to do that? Why won't you show me the photos from the work dinner? You keep talking about there being a problem with them, but what is it?"

Daniel fought hard to rein in his runaway breathing. "What do I have to do to prove—"

"I went to the film lab to find out what the problem is, but Simon wouldn't give me copies."

The stampede of Daniel's anger ran headfirst into that wall of revelation. His voice dropped to a whisper. "You what?"

"Strange guy at first, but he has a real passion for honesty."

Kelly had met Simon? Daniel's voice stayed low, his ears almost ringing with the explosion that mental grenade had created. "What did he say about the photos?"

"That he couldn't give them to me because of some nonsense about a sacred contract with you."

Relief. Simon's eccentricity was a good thing. Finally.

Thirty

Kelly thumbed through Jasmine's message, each word cutting another inch deep into her. "Your name is mud here. Arnold is using it to describe people who aren't Rubicon team players. And he's reading your contract with a fine-tooth comb to see if he can take things further. Take care, hon, and get a lawyer if you haven't already."

Competing images flashed in her mind on an ever-accelerating carousel of confusion. Sick children. Her destroyed reputation. Sick children. A hammer flashing down on a For Sale sign out in front of her dream home. Sick children.

Kelly had to know if she had made the right decision. She turned to Milly, who was in the passenger seat, engrossed in her phone. "You wait here. I'll be back in a minute."

Milly nodded without even looking up. She was adamant she couldn't go to school. Years ago she would have crawled over broken glass rather than miss out on time with her friends. Now she wanted to stay home, and she didn't look sick.

As the little bell announced Kelly's arrival, the back of the lab filled with whirring and clicking. She beelined to the photos on the wall and stood in front of the ornate gold frame. The two children still lay back on hospital beds, their parents in anguish. What had she been thinking? That these photos would somehow give her the answer to the question that had tormented her since she marched out of the elevator at Rubicon Pharma?

Have I done the right thing?

The top corner of the photo shuddered and shimmered. Kelly peered at the red Get Well balloons. Did they move?

They more than moved. The balloons shimmied before the red faded, leaving just a light gray. Kelly's eyes widened as the color from the rest of the photograph drained away. It was as if someone had pulled a plug at the bottom of the frame. She stared—scared—but then turned at the bell's jingle.

Simon cocked his head, studying her. "You look different, Kelly. Lighter almost, like there's a weight lifted from you."

Kelly pointed to the photo of the children. "I'm not sure. But look."

Simon rushed up to the gold frame, a squeal escaping him. "Congratulations!"

In the midst of Kelly's fear emerged a calmness. "What is happening?"

"My photographs show truth—true honesty— in vivid color to grab attention. Bright and gaudy is needed in today's world, but when the attention is no longer needed"—he brushed a finger across the photo frame—"then the color fades."

To Kelly's consternation, the picture dissolved, leaving just an empty frame.

Simon pursed quivering lips. "Your life will be better with this honesty."

"I don't know about that. I lost my job."

"There will always be consequences for honesty in business, but you would have lost more if you hadn't faced this."

Kelly looked over Simon's shoulder at the empty frame. "How did you do that? Is it a digital frame?"

With a light chuckle on his lips, Simon lifted the frame from the wall and held it in front of himself. No wires.

Kelly chewed on her lip and looked out the window. Milly sat staring back at her, a frozen tableau of preteen impatience. Kelly turned to Simon. "Could these frames show me what's going on with my daughter?"

"Why do you need a frame for that?"

Kelly's voice caught in her throat. "Because she's closed off to me and won't talk about anything."

Simon gave a sad nod.

"She's withdrawn into herself, but I can see she's hurting. You don't have a way I can see what's going on with her, do you?"

Simon stared over Kelly's shoulder at Milly. His eyes warmed, and a gentle smile crept across his face. "Truth is something shared, not forced. Sometimes the best way to help others is to help yourself. There are flow-on effects when you face your own truth. Maybe that's what your daughter needs. You might need to guide her as I am guiding you."

"But I've already dealt with—"

"Come." Simon took her elbow. Next to the empty frame was a simple mahogany frame holding a photograph of a bright-pink suitcase sitting next to a home's front door, waiting for its owner.

Kelly stared at it. A suitcase?

"Let me tell you about this truth. The woman is thinking of leaving her partner rather than dealing with their issues so they can mend their relationship and make it stronger."

Kelly jumped to defend a kindred spirit; a woman with whom she sympathized. "Maybe . . . maybe it's because her husband won't listen. Or because they no longer have common ground on which to meet. That happens to a lot of people today, right?"

"It has happened to a lot of people forever. But today more people make this decision as if there are no consequences to their actions, and they won't be guided any other way."

Kelly looked out the window. Milly had drawn

her knees up under her chin and rested her head on her arms. Her consequence.

"What is this place?"

Simon rose on the balls of his feet. "It's a film lab. A place the world says it doesn't need anymore because it can handle things itself. Yet it's needed more than ever. It's an anachronism in a modern world. Like truth itself."

Kelly stared at the empty frame next to the one with the pink suitcase. "We don't connect. Daniel doesn't talk about anything, and I feel like he's holding back from me." She had to try one last time. "There has to be something in his photos. Perhaps it's truth. Simon, can't you at least let me see what's in them?"

Simon frowned. "Not without the sacred contract I have with Daniel. But I can give you something."

Kelly's hopes rose as an answer to the pain of the distance within her family dangled tantalizingly in front of her. "Anything, please."

Simon smiled. "I can give you something more valuable. Freedom."

"Freedom from what?" Kelly's gut kinked into its first tight twist.

"You need to deal with more truth."

The kink tightened into a knot.

Simon raised a finger to the empty frame. "You want your husband to be honest with you, but you aren't honest with him. Perhaps the truth is you aren't sick of him; you're sick of what you've got."

The empty frame sparkled and glittered as a photograph filled in. First, a single sheet of paper, a logo on it familiar to her but not to her husband. The reason she had chosen that bank. Then a statement from Beyond Bank. At first a light gray and then the permanence of black ink. And a name and address. Both belonged to her.

Kelly stared openmouthed. Simon's voice surrounded her. Teased her ears.

"I know you think this is a secret that shouldn't hurt anybody, but it will."

Kelly's wide-eyed amazement morphed into horror as the background of the photograph filled in. Her foyer tiles. The glossy white of her expansive front door. The bank statement sat on top of a suitcase in a red faux alligator print. The suitcase she'd packed and unpacked in her mind many times over. Her own.

"You realize why this suitcase is in bright color, don't you?"

Kelly did.

Thirty-One

Daniel held fate in his hands. It deserved to be tempted.

As he leaned back in his office chair, his thumb brushed the inscription on the base of Gramps's camera, the wording Simon and Gramps had "discussed." *The camera never lies.*

He hoped that was the case this time as well. The Byrnes had been seeing him for a few weeks, and while Sharon had already admitted to an affair with David's best friend, David had jammed the door shut on whatever kept the fires of his anger stoked.

That ruby-red smile appeared at his office door. It was good that Monique was back. One less fire to extinguish. "Your eleven thirty is here."

Daniel placed Gramps's camera on his desk and stood to welcome his clients.

David's anger stormed in before he did, followed by a perfunctory handshake, thunder raging behind his gruff hello. His expression was always a giveaway to the timbre of discussion they would have. Today would be a long hour.

Sharon gave Daniel a tired smile before sitting down in one of the two chairs while David plopped into the other. Their first twenty minutes would be spent defusing whatever bomb had been activated on their drive to the appointment.

"Great to see both of you. Before we start, I'm taking photos of our clients so the team can get to know you. Would you mind?"

The clouds darkened on David's face as he twisted his wedding ring. With a sweet smile, Sharon leaned across the gulf between their chairs.

Daniel turned to pick up the camera, but it was gone.

"There a problem, Daniel?" A menacing triumph rang in David's voice.

Daniel lifted folders and tilted photo frames while he swung frantic glances around his desk. "My camera was here a moment ago."

Sharon pointed to his desk. "Your phone is right there. Why not just use that?"

Daniel stood back from his desk at a complete loss. Had Monique picked it up?

David's fingers rapped an angry tattoo on his armrest. "Just use your phone! I've got a job interview straight after this."

Daniel reached for his phone, defeated and angry. He held it up with a limp enthusiasm as Sharon offered another smile. David traded his scowl for a sarcastic grin.

Daniel flopped into his chair as the couple looked to him to start their conversation. He threw surreptitious glances left and right—

where was it? He had to get his head back in the game, and he blinked hard to reengage with the crumbling marriage in front of him. He shoved aside the confusion over the camera and grabbed a notepad, ready to save another marriage with no extra help.

"So that's the best advice you've got? Open up? Hold no secrets?" David tapped an angry finger on his cheek as he slouched in his chair. "I could get that from ten minutes of watching Dr. Phil, and it would also save me a fortune."

Daniel was expecting this. Again the topic of David's baggage had come up, and again he'd slammed the door shut on any discussion about it.

David leaned forward, elbows perched on his knees, and sneered in Daniel's direction. "She said you were a hotshot counselor with a bestselling book. Bestselling? Where did you get that information?"

A crack scooted down Daniel's self-control, and an ear-splitting shatter echoed in his head. "How dare you!"

David sat stunned, not expecting his bait to be swallowed.

The veins in Daniel's neck throbbed as he pointed an angry finger at the man who was now retreating into his chair. "You come in here, full of righteous anger and unforgiveness you clearly enjoy, unwilling to accept any responsibility for your life. You reject the heartfelt apology from your wife and put her through extra hell while you force her to suffer the fallout from your inability to take responsibility for yourself."

Sharon blinked hard at Daniel. David's chest resumed its heaving.

Daniel eased away from his clients, trying desperately to screw a lid back on his famed self-control.

Two words burst from David as he stood in a rush, and then he disappeared into the corridor in a huff.

An apology formed on Daniel's lips, but it hung there, unuttered, as Sharon burst into tears.

"Thanks, I guess, for what I'll be dealing with for the next week. I thought you could help us." She gathered her handbag, sobs racking her body as she slunk from his office.

The horror of his behavior numbed him, and he stared at the doorway. Daniel had never lost a client, but now that copybook was well and truly blotted.

He heard a bright knock on his door. Monique appeared, balancing a steaming mug of coffee and a muffin the size of a bowling ball. "Have you got a moment to talk?"

"Not now, Monique."

Her lower lip quivered. "I made this for you. I know how much great cooking means to you."

She placed her gifts on his desk and took a seat on the couch. "We need to talk."

Daniel clenched his jaw. "Now is not a good time."

She recrossed long legs. "Is there anything I can do for you?"

Another wave of anger crested over him. He needed some space, some air. "Not at the moment."

She leaned forward, and a waft of Chanel drifted over to him. "I understand you, Daniel, and I can see you need to talk. Talk to me."

Daniel closed his eyes, his pulse pounding. "I *said* not now, Monique!" He opened his eyes to an empty sofa. Sobs filtered in from the corridor. What else could go wrong?

The sobs were replaced by the ring of the practice switchboard. A second ring. A third. Monique never let it get to four. Another ring. Then a fifth.

The light flashed impatiently on his phone. It was probably best if she didn't take the call in the state she was in. He punched at the light. "Welcome to Crossroads Counseling. This is Daniel Whiteley."

The briefest hesitation. "Daniel? Amanda Porter. Are you answering your own phones nowadays?"

Daniel forced a laugh, which he regretted in an instant. "I think I know why you're calling."

A beat of silence on the other end of the conversation disagreed. "I'm not sure you do." Amanda's voice wasn't serving its usual dollops of encouragement. It was flatter. Steelier. More knife than spoon.

"You're after the ideas for my next book, and it's coming together a little slower than I wanted."

"I'm calling to request our advance back."

Daniel's future rolled up in front of him like retracting blinds pulled too quickly. The house. His business. His reputation. His family.

"We've reached that point now where we need to move on. In truth, we passed it a long time ago."

Daniel's breathing grew ragged and shallow. "Can't you give me a little more time? I think in another two weeks I'll be able to—"

"It's been months. How will another two weeks help?"

"You don't understand. The advance has gone toward the house—"

The steel in Amanda's voice sharpened. "How you manage money is not our responsibility, but we are in the business of managing ours."

A heavy sigh. "I see."

"I'm sorry it didn't work out. Sometimes first-time authors stumble across a great idea but they can't follow it up."

The anxiety of his unspoken secret blossomed

into terrifying life. Handing back the advance meant he'd lose his house. If he came clean about *No Secrets* coming from Howard, he would lose a lot more than that. He signed off and cut the call.

He saw movement in his office doorway. Anna slipped into his office and closed the door behind her. "We need to talk."

What now?

She sat down heavily on Daniel's couch and stared at the carpet, wringing her hands as if ordering her thoughts. "I'll get straight to it. I've overheard everything this morning. The yelling match with your client. That conversation with your editor. What's going on?"

The idea of finding sweet relief in a shared burden toyed with him, but pride wouldn't let the words come. As each second ticked away, he realized Anna was studying him from behind that raised eyebrow and analyzing his silence. Goodness knew he'd done the same thing enough times.

He laced his fingers behind his head. "I'm behind on the deadline for my next book."

"By how much?"

"Nearly twelve months."

Anna's second eyebrow shot up to join the first. "Twelve months? How could you possibly be that far behind?"

Her silence doled out enough rope for Daniel to

either climb out of the hole he found himself in or hang himself. Ghosts of couples past chuckled as he got a taste of what it was like to sit in his office with someone else pulling the strings of the conversation.

"It's taking me longer than I first thought."

Daniel knew how the mechanics of silence worked, but now he appreciated why.

"No kidding, but I don't think you're being honest with me."

Daniel wanted to fill the silence but was tackled by a sense of pride, unwilling to be cut down to size.

Anna's voice cracked as it rose. "Why won't you tell me? Why is it so hard for a bestselling author to write another book?"

He had to be honest with her, at the very least to release the pressure pounding inside his head. But that release came with a huge price. Several huge prices.

"And what's going on with your house?"

At last, a question with an easy answer.

"They want their advance back. That was our down payment, and without another book, we can't keep it."

Anna's brow furrowed, her silence extracting answers from Daniel. Answers he did not want to hear out loud. This had to end.

"Anna, I can't deal with this right now. Trust me, I'll fix it."

The confusion on Anna's face was at odds with her nod. "We also need to talk about Monique. She's back at work, but she's been erratic and rude with some clients. I've talked to her, and she's planning to take stress leave. By the sound of her conversation with you, just in time."

Daniel breathed easier. At least one problem had an easy solution. "It's probably best."

Anna drew in a sharp breath. "Is it, Daniel?" Her voice shook with a quiet rage. "Did you hear what I said? She's taking *stress* leave. If it looks at all like you're responsible, the practice will be on a legal hook if she pursues it. I can't force you to do anything, but you need to do something. And now it's more than for your own sake; it's for all our sakes. Take a day off, clear your head, and sort things out. I'll cover for you here. Go for a walk right now and take some photos with that camera Gramps gave you." She nodded toward his desk.

Daniel spun in his chair. Gramps's camera sat next to the photo frames, its single, unblinking eye staring him down.

Thirty-Two

Kelly stared into her own eyes, eyes from an age ago. Eyes sparkling love in the present and hope in the future. On her young cheeks was a rosy sheen she hadn't seen in some time, and her slender, wine-bottle neck swept down to a figure she'd spent too long trying to hide because she was convinced it wasn't worth looking at. How wrong she was back then.

But her eyes held the biggest change.

Next to her in the wedding photo was a loving glance above a goofy grin from a tuxedoed Daniel, tall and proud. Neither of those traits had changed. They held hands in the sunset, and she saw the one thing she missed most. Connection.

Kelly straightened their wedding photo and brought her living room back to order. Ruffled cushions arranged on the leather sofa. Magazines fanned on the coffee table. She tried to conjure happy memories, times when her dream home had delivered dreams.

Memories of happier times trickled back. A four-year-old Milly telling her looping, interminable stories, keeping her parents in stitches with extra detail that required a reboot of the entire story with each addition. Providing the audience for a serious seven-year-old's dance recital in a homemade newspaper crown. As the stories unfolded, the brush of her memory painted in the background. The sofa was brown velour, not gray leather. The room was small, not expansive with views to the ocean.

The memories were not of this house.

The happier times rolled on. Gramps's eightieth birthday, Kelly's Cajun dishes a hit. Milly's squeals of delight, her tiny cheeks glowing from the candlelight on the teddy bear cake that had kept Kelly up until midnight.

She looked across to the sparkling glass and gleaming silver of her expansive kitchen. These memories didn't take place there. All her happiness had taken place somewhere else, somewhen else. Not now. Not here. Here was defined more and more by awkward silences, unfulfilled dreams, and Milly's refusal to come out of her room.

She had to be honest with Daniel.

Leaving might put some distance between her and the pain of the present, but it wouldn't return her to those times—times she would revisit in a heartbeat. And she didn't want to leave. She had cried over coffee with Jasmine about the breakdown of her marriage and her family. Still, it was not a place she wanted to be. The thought of leaving had toyed with her in moments of frustration with her husband but had taken root when the first seeds of suspicion were planted. They were watered by the realization that the distance between them wasn't busyness, that there might be more to it. When she felt the best way to win a debate with Daniel was to hold an unspoken one in her own head.

But still the suspicion clung to her—unless she was clinging to it.

Maybe Jasmine was right; she should just threaten to leave. But Simon's point jabbed into her conscience. If she expected Daniel to be honest with her, she had to be honest with him— and with herself.

She just had to pick the right moment to talk to Daniel.

Her phone rang. Kelly looked across at the screen, hoping it wasn't her husband. Not now, in the middle of these unordered thoughts. A sinking feeling grew in the pit of her stomach. The phone number was Milly's school.

"Mrs. Whiteley, Nicholas Rhodes from St. Arcadia's Academy. How are you?"

Milly's principal. Kelly pumped energy into her end of the conversation to fight a rising dread. "Fine, thank you."

"Mrs. Whiteley—Kelly—I don't like making calls like this, but it's an important one to make. We have identified your daughter as being at risk. Milly blurted to her teacher that things are so bad at home she'll need to do something drastic to get your attention."

Kelly jammed her eyes shut, horrified. *At risk* was bad enough. *Your daughter* made it so much worse.

"It's in Milly's best interest for you to come in and talk with us."

Kelly fought hard to lasso her stampeding breathing. "Anything to help Milly talk would be good."

The principal gave a light chuckle. "Of course, I don't need to tell your husband that. We have counselors here, but if you'd prefer to have that conversation with someone away from our school, I'm sure your husband knows someone who can help."

He did. Anna. But Kelly would not outsource mothering her daughter to Daniel's work-wife.

"Actually, how is Daniel? He missed our regular at-risk teens counseling session yesterday. I hope he's okay."

Daniel never missed an appointment. Time slowed to molasses as she booked an appointment with her daughter's school to intervene. To save her life. A failed mother, that's what she felt like, and she was sick of feeling it.

She needed to text Daniel with the time for the principal meeting. No, she'd talk to him about it. He could rearrange his schedule. Their daughter was suffering and acting out. Staying together for Milly's sake wasn't working. It was making her worse, and while Daniel could pretend to the outside world that everything was fine, maybe it would take something like this to get him to see someone. Now.

And if he didn't want to, there was only one thing left to do.

Thirty-Three

Daniel's reflection stared back at him with a tired resignation. He should be anywhere but here. His first day off in three years, and a nagging thought had chipped away at him all night. And it had won.

Daniel leaned on the glass door, and the tiny bell jingled his arrival. The film processor whirred and clunked in the back of the lab as the waft of chemicals drifted over the counter and grabbed him in an acrid grip.

He noticed two new cameras on the shelf, each from a time before technology, each with a fluttering price tag. He checked his watch. For the first time in a long time, he wasn't in a hurry to be somewhere else, but this urgency was greater. Far greater.

The eerie familiarity of one colorful photo in a mahogany frame drew him across the film lab in a rush. Was that Kelly's suitcase? He stared hard. The tiles in his own foyer were unmistakable. The first bubble of anger bobbled its way to the surface. He hadn't given Simon permission to put his family on display.

Daniel shuffled along the frames, crouching and then standing on tiptoes, checking each for signs of a violation of his privacy. None of the photos were his. He reached a large pine frame just behind the counter and skidded to a halt. The frame was no longer empty.

The tiny bell jingled as Simon entered, steam rising from the Chinese takeout container swinging from his fingers.

Daniel's pulse thudded in his ears as he thrust a quivering finger at the frame. "What do you call this?"

Simon placed his lunch on the counter. "The honest truth."

Daniel breathed ragged and hard, seething anger sizzling as he rushed at Simon, grinding a finger hard into his chest. "You don't have my permission to put a photo of my book up on display."

"Haven't you built a business on the back of telling people to come clean with each other and hold no secrets?"

White-hot flashes of rage and confusion clashed for control of Daniel. "I demand you take it down now!"

"It's not so easy when it's you, is it? And you should know there's only one way to get rid of it. Let me help you bring the life back to . . . well, your life." Simon leaned into the savory steam that billowed from his lunch. "Mr. Ming's steamed dim sims are to die for, aren't they?"

Molten anger spewed out of Daniel as he stomped over to the frame. He wrenched it from the wall and tore the photograph from it, crumpling it in his hand and letting it fall to the floor. "The only way, hey?"

Simon gave a sad nod toward the frame in Daniel's hands.

At first there was a vibration in Daniel's palms and then a hammering. The wood grew warm as the frame filled in with the sheer white of photographic paper. An invisible hand drew in the edges of a rectangular object and then detail. Words appeared in thick, black, chunky letters, and then a photo of a book, its title proud. But then the invisible hand stopped, not adding the author's name.

Daniel dropped the frame with a scream and sprinted to the door. He flung it open, mashing the tiny bell against the wall. Simon's yell followed him into the street. "You need to face them, Daniel!"

Daniel's tires crunched on the gravel of his driveway. Magical cameras that appeared at will. Photos that couldn't be destroyed. He had to end this.

He ran through the foyer and skidded to a stop as he entered the kitchen. Kelly leaned against the counter, inspecting Gramps's camera as she turned it over in her hands.

Daniel's anger dizzied him. "So now you go through my stuff?"

"*My* stuff? You left the camera out here on the kitchen counter."

No, I didn't. "So you broke into Gramps's briefcase."

"I don't even know where the briefcase is. Daniel, I am telling you the truth. I came home, and the camera was sitting here."

No, it wasn't.

Kelly placed the camera on the counter and spun to face him, eyes filling with angry tears. "Speaking of the truth, where were you today? I rang the office, and they said you hadn't come in. And then Jade said Monique wasn't in either—"

Her pleas were white noise, background to one question: How did she get the camera? Daniel stormed past her and into the study. The briefcase sat in the bottom of his closet, pushed toward the back. He checked the tumblers: still out of sync, the clasps unmoving. He staggered back into the kitchen.

"Did you even hear what I said? And why don't you believe me? I thought you left it out because the film was used up."

Daniel reeled, punch-drunk at the flurry of blows tipping up everything he thought he knew. "That's impossible."

"Do you want me to take the film to Simon?"

One blow too many. A giant crack split his resolve down the middle. He snatched the camera from the counter and sprinted, huffing and heaving, to the deck.

Kelly raced after him. "What is going on—"

Daniel stood at the railing as he cradled the camera in his trembling hands. One single letter burned into his retinas. In the tiny plastic window on top of the camera was a red *F*. The camera was full. All the photographs had been taken.

There was only one thing to do.

With a primal scream born of weeks—months—of frustration and hurt, he ripped open the back of the camera and tore the film from its canister. He flung it from the deck, the ribbon of film trailing behind the tiny canister like a comet's tail as it fell to the rocks below.

Kelly screamed. "Daniel! What are you doing?"

He took a final look at the camera, the last memory of Gramps, and threw back his arm.

"Daniel! No!"

His guttural scream exploded from the cliff top as the camera arced into the air, rose above the horizon, and kissed the afternoon sun before falling. First into the azure background of a wide ocean, and then tumbling, tumbling to the rocks two hundred feet below.

Daniel rushed to the handrail to see Gramps's last gift to him explode into a cloud of plastic and dust. A split second later, a tiny crash reached his ears.

Then silence, save for the pulsing sobs of his wife.

Thirty-Four

The stream of water shimmied and shook its way into Kelly's glass. On the other side of the doors to their deck, Daniel bent over the railing, his back heaving.

She couldn't keep going like this, carrying their burden on her own. They had to see someone, and if Daniel chose his reputation over their happiness, she would leave. It would devastate Milly, but that was Daniel's decision. It wasn't ideal, but it was better than tiptoeing through the minefield in which they currently lived.

Kelly downed the water in one long, shaky gulp. Then her heart pounded as she slid back the glass doors and her heels clattered onto the deck. She plunged into a conversation that was long overdue. "What was all that about?"

Daniel threw back his head, and Kelly steeled herself for anger. For explanation. She was unprepared for what she got.

With one almighty groan, Daniel dissolved into sobs. Her tower of strength crumbled before her eyes and mumbled of ruin. His filmed eyes flitted around the deck, searching for the starting point of an answer.

Kelly took two hesitant steps forward. "Talk

to me like you used to. It doesn't matter where you start." She gave him a moment to compose himself as he sucked in huge breaths and ran a trembling hand through his thick, curly hair.

His voice came at an almost whisper. "I can't stop it."

Kelly's thoughts hurtled to their usual self-destroying conclusion. Another woman. Or an addiction he'd swept under the carpet.

Daniel took a blubbering breath. "First it was the gift of cuff links—"

The confirmation of another woman didn't bring a sense of closure. Instead it swept aside Kelly's confidence in a jet of rejection.

"And then holding hands with Anna here on the deck—" Sobs stole the last of his sentence, and he paced the deck.

Something inside Kelly shattered. The work-wife. She should have known. She flicked through her memory for warning signs, but the attempt was swallowed by a rising anger. With him. With Anna. With herself for suspecting but doing nothing about it. But she had to let him talk. She had spent the last however many months wishing he would, and she couldn't stop him now.

"And Howard's legacy—" Daniel spun on his heel and all but collapsed on the railing.

Her husband's gushing honesty both relieved and scared her. The locked-down control she leaned on was gone, but the door to his heart wasn't really open; it merely swung wildly, clinging to exploded hinges. Why was he talking about Howard?

"But the one I don't understand is your suitcase and that statement from Beyond Bank."

Kelly froze. Daniel's words hung on the ocean breeze that flitted across the deck as the secret she'd tried to hide for some time was breathed into life. Now it sat between them.

Daniel shook his head as if trying to regain control. "You probably think I'm crazy." He looked down to her, in his eyes a sense of something foreign. Imploring. Like Milly looked whenever she argued for the sake of it but needed to know if it was safe to do so.

"I don't think you're crazy." Kelly breathed deep, summoning courage. "And I can explain the bank statement."

Daniel was a tableau of stillness. The only movement, his eyes.

Kelly gulped in another breath of courage. "Simon told me that if I want you to be honest with me, I need to be honest with you. I've been thinking about leaving you."

Daniel's shoulders slumped.

"The reason for the suitcase appearing in the photos is probably because I packed and unpacked it several times in my mind, but I only got as far as the front door."

Daniel continued to sag, and for the first time in a long time, he seemed to be speechless.

"And although I always calmed down, inevitably there would be another fight, and in my mind I'd pull the suitcase from my closet and pack it." Kelly prepared herself for anger. A counterargument. Anything. A light wind drifted across their deck.

"Simon's photos show truth. I imagine the suitcase represents that I've wanted to leave you. Over and over again."

Daniel stared, the breeze ruffling his hair. Kelly rushed forward to grab his arm. "Gramps's camera is real, Daniel. Simon showed me the truth in those photos."

Daniel blanched as he covered his mouth. "He showed you?"

"Not our photos. Apparently you have some kind of sacred contract with him. But I think we need to look at this as an opportunity and look at our photos together—"

The Beatles interrupted them as notes from a plaintive guitar and a nasally George Harrison burst from his pocket. "Listen . . . do you want to know a secret?" Kelly willed Daniel to ignore his phone and lost. Again.

Daniel snatched at his phone, his posture reinflating at the recognition of the name. Her husband transformed into the professional Daniel, his breathing now under control, his eyes narrowed. Their connection was severed as he stood at his full height. "Principal Rhodes, what can I do for you?"

Daniel forced a wince from his face.

"Uh, yes, something came up, and I couldn't make the at-risk program . . . No, there's no problem. My apologies. I should have had Monique let you know."

Kelly took tentative steps away from her husband. She hadn't told him about the principal's call. She hadn't had the chance.

Daniel reached out to her. "That's news to me. I didn't know about it."

Kelly burned under the heat of her husband's spotlight gaze. *No, you wouldn't, Daniel. I couldn't tell you about our daughter because you were throwing cameras off cliffs.*

"We'll talk about it, and I look forward to seeing you then." Daniel cut the call, their burgeoning reconnection cut with it. "Apparently the principal would like us to come in for a formal appointment to discuss Milly's behavior at school. When were you planning to tell me?"

The anger and fear that wriggled under Kelly's self-control exploded into life. "I haven't had the chance to tell you because he just called, and since then we've been out here dealing with whatever you're not telling me." Daniel dropped his head. Now was the time. "We have to go see someone. I can't keep going like this."

"Yes, you've mentioned that before, and I said someone at Crossroads would be happy to work with us—"

"I don't want to go to your work, Daniel. We need to go somewhere where we'll be equals in the conversation."

Daniel sighed deeply. "Okay."

One simple word. Four simple letters. But it had taken him so long to say it.

"I'm willing to talk about finding someone else."

"Why is this such a problem for you? Isn't counseling confidential?"

"Our industry is just like any other. Word would get out. I just know it. The best answer for me would be to see Anna, or even Peter. To keep it in-house. No one will want to see a marriage counselor whose own marriage is falling apart."

Kelly was torn. He had responded to her ultimatum, albeit with conditions. And what he was saying made sense. "We need to do it for Milly. What we're doing—or pretending to have—is hurting her."

Their connection sparked back into weak life, fanned by the joint love of their daughter.

Kelly tried one last time. "So what was that with the camera?"

Daniel stopped, drawing shades over his response. "I'm sorry. I just got . . . angry."

"Why do I get the feeling everything you say is crafted before I hear it?"

"I wish I hadn't done it." But something in his eyes disagreed with that sentiment. He brushed past her. "I have to get out of here for a while."

What was going on inside his head that he refused to talk about? There could be only one answer. Whatever was in his photos was so damning that he had to get rid of the camera. There was a way to find out—Simon. She would just have to convince him. Beg him, if necessary.

Thirty-Five

The whipping tall grass left a vicious sting on Daniel's calves. The white-and-yellow flowers that lined the walking path bent back and forth, their heads struggling against the gale, their faces bent away. Two hundred feet below, waves meandered to the shoreline in a random, messy wash. Pounding surf, eroding rock grain by grain, out of sync but powerful alone. And washing away the last gift Gramps gave him.

Waves of remorse pounded Daniel. Gramps had entrusted him with the one thing in his life that had apparently saved him from himself, and he had destroyed it. Why would Gramps do this to him? He would have to know Daniel would get rid of it. Who wouldn't when faced with the prospect of having their deepest secrets revealed for everyone to see? He threw back his head, the wind sweeping away his screamed apology. "I'm sorry, okay?"

The dirty gray of the clouds smudged the blue from the sky. He had no doubt that, through the camera, those clouds would look white, bursting with light. Was this the lesson Gramps mentioned in his letter? That the world was a different place when you looked through a lens of honesty? When you saw things how they really were? The gift of Gramps's camera wasn't pulling back the rug under which Daniel had swept what he believed was best avoided. The gift was to see the world as it truly was, and he had hurled that gift into the sunset.

Daniel grimaced as his shoulders sank. He had thrown away not only the last of Gramps but the chance to deal with something in his life that wasn't just hidden but eating away at him under the surface.

Why was it so hard to be honest about the book? He encouraged people to open up—hold no secrets—while handing them a book that hid his own. He remembered the prices on the cameras in Simon's Film Lab. Not "Or Best Offer" but "Whatever Is Needed." Was that what this was about?

Daniel thought long and hard about the price he would have to pay for the mistake he'd made. Claiming Howard's manuscript as his own when the bank warned they would close the practice if they couldn't make their payments had seemed so simple. And the price of omission seemed worth paying if it saved the practice. But then he'd discounted it each time he'd drifted into a lie. When the publisher queried his credentials. When the TV morning show asked about his inspiration. When couples flooded into his practice because of the wisdom on pages he hadn't written. Edited, yes. Written, no. And the price had sat in the background, compounding with the interest of each lie, waiting to be paid.

A gust of wind buffeted him from the path. He turned for home as the sun broke through a seam in the clouds, spotlighting the price of honesty. His house would go. Unanswered questions spiraled into a numbing dread. What had Simon said to Kelly? She had seen his photos on the wall—she'd even said the camera was special. And what would the impact be on Milly if they separated?

Daniel weighed his options, a tried-and-true reflex. On one side, confessing his secrets, leading to a failed practice, a ruined reputation, and a broken family. On the other, keeping his silence and bearing the regret at severing his last connection to Gramps. The scales dipped down on the side of a broken future. The price was too high.

He looked again over the waters below, the pounding ocean retreating from rocks strewn with seagrass. His pride curled its finger and enticed him down a familiar, well-trodden path. He would draw a line in the sand and deal with this himself.

The control flooded back with the relief. His

pace quickened along the path as strategies danced in his head. First his marriage and family. He had agreed to talk with Kelly about speaking to another counselor, and while Kelly wouldn't see Anna because of a truth she refused to accept, another option would allow him to keep this in-house—Peter. Anna could talk to Milly just as she had already reached out to do.

Confidence surged through him as he placed his hands back on the wheel of his life. He strode along the path, oblivious to the grass whipping his shins.

That left only one problem unaddressed. His publisher. He would argue his case with Amanda to see if they could give him any extra leeway—any at all—to ease the process of paying back an advance he'd already spent. His breathing resumed a more normal rhythm with shorter, sharper intakes. It had taken him nearly a year to write nothing. How on earth could he deliver something in a matter of weeks? There was only one response to that. He would force the inspiration to come. Maybe Google could inspire him. He'd been gifted enough to take Howard's idea and improve it to the point of publication, so he would just do it again with some other idea he'd find. He'd make it his own.

Daniel broke into a jog. He could do this. His

jog graduated into a sprint, buoyed with if not an escape plan then at least an escape route. He nudged aside the grief over Gramps's camera to be dealt with at a more appropriate time.

He crunched up his driveway and then flung open the front door and brushed past Kelly in the living room.

"Daniel? Can we talk about—"

"Not now, Kel."

Daniel hustled toward his study, firing on all cylinders, fueled by anxiety and adrenaline. He pushed open the door, and his world shattered. Blinding, flashing pain flared behind his eyes.

No!

The camera sat on Gramps's recliner. Daniel slumped against the doorframe and sank to the floor, the last of his resolve melting as the adrenaline ebbed away. It couldn't be. It wasn't, his rational side argued. Stress caused hallucinations—he knew that from the textbooks, and he'd even diagnosed it a number of times in his office.

Daniel crawled on his hands and knees to the chair, expecting the vision of the camera to fade. Instead, its unblinking lens caught the light and sparkled. His fingers clung to the edge of his desk as his eyes popped up next to the camera, a snail checking to see if the bird had gone. It hadn't. Through the window on the back of the camera, Daniel saw film.

Sobs burst from his chest as he slumped back to the floor. He didn't even need to check the tiny letter on top of the camera. He knew all the film had been used.

Thirty-Six

The single lens of the camera bored a hole in Daniel's soul. Accusing, all-knowing. He settled back into Gramps's recliner. Would Gramps have had more than this old chair if he'd dealt with his secrets earlier? If he'd spent his money on something other than—

Daniel bolted upright. Gramps had been a gambler, but there was another reason he'd had nothing. He'd continued to pay for photos, and the price had kept going up.

This was his future. But it didn't have to be.

He thumbed in the combination for Gramps's briefcase and pulled out the photo album. The secrets of others flicked through his fingers. The stiff pages groaned as he saw the photos in a different light. These weren't the wrong moments to take a photo; they were the right ones. He flicked further. The photo of him and Kelly at Milly's party was in full color. Milly at her party, the tears glistening. In full color.

He picked up the camera and brushed his finger across the inscription. *The camera never lies.* If he couldn't get rid of it—and the camera would never lie—he had no choice.

Daniel placed the photo album back in

the briefcase and reached for the words his grandfather left for him. As he read Gramps's letter, the last words took on a different meaning.

I know you've got great insights into other people, but I worry for your family, Daniel. When I've raised this before, you've always shifted the conversation.

In that moment, Daniel appreciated the reason Gramps had given the camera to him and not to his mother. This was the only way to get through to him. He wished Gramps were alive so he could at least tell him *why* he had shifted the conversation. It wasn't because he thought he knew better; it was because of the shame of having his hero know his flaws. He didn't want to be less than perfect in his grandfather's eyes. But Gramps had seen so much more than Daniel ever imagined, and that was worse. He had presented a successful facade to Gramps so he would think him a success, but with his insight, he could see just how much of a fake Daniel was.

If only he'd listened.

Would Milly be happier? Would Kelly? Would they even have their dream house? Probably not, but they would have something even more valuable.

> Forgive an old man for advising the counselor, but I can see where your hearts are and where you're headed. Based on your current trajectory, I'm not sure you'll last.

So the whole time Gramps could see what their problem was, but Daniel was too proud to accept his help.

Daniel scanned the rest of the letter.

> I can help. I'm leaving you this gift I wish I had in my younger days, when choices in front of me were easier and would have saved so much pain . . . Please use it wisely; it has freed me from so much and taught me there's always more to life than what we see.

He knew what he needed to do.

Daniel splayed his fingers on Simon's counter, a deadweight bow in his shoulders, his heart heavy. A single, tiny film canister sat in front of him.

Simon stroked his chin. "Didn't I say it would be easier to come clean about your secrets? I know what's on this film."

A tired sigh escaped from Daniel. "What?"

"Truth. Inescapable truth."

Inescapable. "When will they be ready?"

"In an hour."

An hour. The usual length of a counseling session. Daniel always expected that the couple in front of him would commit to accepting the truth he'd spotlighted for them within that hour. Now, standing in the first seconds of an hour, he realized just how long sixty minutes could be.

"That will be fifty-five dollars."

Daniel's blood thumped in his ears. "Fifty-five? For developing my photos in an hour? It was only thirty-three dollars the first time and forty-four after that! This is extortion!"

A warmth filled Simon's eyes. "Surely you of all people know that the price is always higher the longer secrets remain."

Incredible. "You can't do this!"

Instead of defense, there was an understanding, a compassion, but no backing down from the price. Daniel meekly reached for his wallet.

"You think the price today is high? Wait until your secrets fester even longer."

Daniel flicked a glance at the frames on the wall, faces caught in a moment, their pain visible to all. And his book still on display at the end of the row.

Simon picked up the film canister with white-gloved fingers. "I'm so pleased you want to see who you are rather than who you want others to think you are. I'll see you in an hour." He shuffled to the back of the lab and creaked open a door on the side of the huge film processor.

The tiny bell jingled Daniel's arrival back into the real world. What was real, anyway? What we see? Or what is just behind it?

A woman dressed in Lycra powered toward him, a screaming child in the stroller she pushed between heavy breaths. She threw Daniel a sweet smile as she passed him, but it slipped as she resumed her pace. A Lexus cruised past, a meaty, hairy arm resting in the open window, two-hundred-dollar sunglasses nodding to the pounding drum and bass. Was that Lexus a hard-earned luxury? Or a ball and chain, trapping the driver under a mirage of wealth propped up by shaky financing?

Almost on autopilot, Daniel trudged up Northbound Avenue, the homing beacon of work drawing him in. Like it did most days. He had an hour to kill and nowhere else to go.

Thirty-Seven

Daniel's entry to the practice was greeted by neither a ruby-red smile nor a flirty hello. The reception desk was as empty as the wall opposite. Silence filled the offices of Crossroads, an eerie portent into a future of consequences when he'd be run out of the industry as a fraud because the guy behind the bestselling book *No Secrets* had kept a secret of his own. A big one.

A brunette head with a burgundy streak poked around the corner. "Daniel! What are you doing here?"

Words deserted him. He didn't know.

"You look terrible! Are you okay?"

Another question without an answer. "Where's Monique?"

"I don't know. I can't reach her."

An uncomfortable silence descended on them like a thick theater curtain. Two professionals stared at each other, as if actors waiting for each other to deliver the next line.

Anna's burgundy streak shook. "What's going on?"

Daniel smiled, tight-lipped. He would have to face the truth, and he needed to start somewhere. "My life is falling apart."

Anna ushered him to the sofa, her practiced silence deafening.

"We have to see the principal about Milly's behavior. She's talked of hurting herself at school."

Anna's eyes widened. "Hurting herself?"

Daniel massaged his temples, again faced with a question to which honesty was the only answer. "She told the school she needs to do something drastic to get our attention, and that's their conclusion. Mine too."

"She never mentioned that to me when we talked."

"It's more than that . . . Kelly's planning on leaving me. She's even opened her own bank account."

Anna winced. "Why don't you both talk to one of us?"

"Kelly won't. She's convinced there's something going on with me and . . . someone else."

"With Monique?"

The anxiety launched a fresh assault on him.

"Why would she suspect there's someone else?" Anna inspected his expression. "Have you given her a reason to think there's something going on?"

Daniel blinked hard. "Not consciously."

"Then talk to someone else. You can still fix this, but you can't be the divorced guy who wrote the book on staying happily married."

Daniel's jaw rippled as he closed the cover on his emotions.

Anna leaned toward him, her eyebrow cocked. "Every time I mention your book, you shut down. You used to be happy to talk about anything and everything."

Daniel stared off into space. "You'd think I was crazy."

Anna's second eyebrow joined her first. "I've heard them all. Try me."

"We all have secrets, Anna, and part of their deceptive beauty is the fact that we think we can keep them to ourselves until we're ready for the right moment . . ." Daniel let his sentence trail into the ether.

"I've read chapter one in your book. We all have."

Daniel blinked back tears. "But what if your secrets were revealed for you, and you couldn't stop it?"

Anna simply stared.

The crack in Daniel's voice spread, carried on a tide of anxiety. "And what if you're being taunted with photographs of your secrets waved under your nose, laying bare what you'd prefer to leave tucked away in the darkness?"

Anna's eyes widened. "Photographs? Is this why you can't show me the photo from our dinner?"

The fuse that had been lit in Simon's Film

Lab reached his fragile self-control, and Daniel exploded. He jumped to his feet, his voice shrieking from him. "I can't stop it. Do you hear me?"

He flung open the door and sprinted from the practice, leaving Anna standing in a reception area without a group photo, a receptionist, or a business partner.

Thirty-Eight

Kelly's knee bounced in time with the ticking clock that carved off the seconds outside Principal Rhodes's office. Her call to Daniel went to voice mail for the third time in five minutes. There was no point leaving another message. She shook her head at the elderly woman behind the counter and received back an unamused smile.

She had to find out what was going on with her husband. She speed-dialed another familiar number.

"Crossroads Counseling. This is Jade."

"Jade, it's Kelly Whiteley—"

"So wonderful to speak with you! Thank you so much for the warm hospitality and your amazing food. You have all been wonderful to me in a difficult time—"

Kelly laid out the pieces for the conversation she would have to have, as difficult as it might be.

"—but I'm afraid you've just missed Daniel."

Kelly took a giant breath, more than anything to inflate her confidence so she could speak to the person who—and this cut deep to even acknowledge—knew Daniel better than anyone.

"That's okay. I'm not calling for Daniel. Could you put me through to Anna, please?"

"One moment."

Simon would be no help without whatever this sacred contract was. Only one option was left.

The on-hold music cut with an abrupt jolt. "Kelly, I'm glad you've called. I'm worried about Daniel."

The first wave in her plan of attack stalled before it began as Anna stole Kelly's opening line. "Looks like we both are." She summoned forward her first line of attack troops, although now it felt more like defense. She turned away from the counter and cupped her hand around the phone as her voice dropped into a whisper. "First, I need to clear the air between me and Daniel's work."

A practiced silence. Professional. There was no other way to say it than to just get to the point. "Anna, is Daniel cheating behind my back with anyone at work?"

She braced herself for a defensive justification or a changing of the subject. She got neither.

"No, he isn't."

The answer to a question that drained her of emotional energy forced her voice into a whisper. "Thank you."

"I'm a little put out you thought you needed to ask me."

"I had to ask. Daniel spends so much time

buried in work, and he no longer talks at home."

"He's expressed frustration to me a number of times, saying he has answered that question but you didn't want to listen."

Kelly winced. That stung. It was hard to bat away criticism when it was wrapped around a kernel of truth. "I just want us to be like we used to be."

"I wish that for you as well, Kelly. You and Daniel need to talk to someone."

"When I suggested that we talk to someone— perhaps not at Crossroads—Daniel got defensive and refused."

"I can see why."

"But—"

"He was protecting his reputation, which, at one level, is fair. Would you get a builder to build your new home if you discovered his own house was falling apart?"

No, she wouldn't.

"So maybe remember that when you two talk about what to do next. I'm more than willing to help. But regardless of what you do, I encourage you to do it fast."

"Why? What's happened?"

"Daniel just left here ranting about secrets that appeared in photographs—"

Photographs.

"—and he scared me. Daniel has always been a rational, in-control guy. I've never seen him like this. And when I asked him about the group photo, the one we took on your deck, he exploded and ran out."

Kelly felt a growing reaction—an old, familiar one. A compassion for the man she loved. He wasn't concealing another woman; he was genuinely in trouble.

"He was talking about secrets being waved around like photos. I've got no idea what he was talking about."

Kelly did.

"Gramps's camera. It's special."

"How could it be special?"

"I'm about to find out. Did Daniel ever show you a contract he had with the guy who develops his photos?"

An impolite throat cleared from over her shoulder. Kelly looked up into the disapproving gaze of the elderly gatekeeper to the academy's seat of power, flicking glances to the clock on the wall like ninja stars. "I'm sorry, Mrs. Whiteley, but the principal can't wait any longer for your husband. He'll see you now or not at all. At least not today."

Kelly closed the last drawer in Daniel's filing cabinet. She'd found no paperwork carrying a Simon's Film Lab logo or anything remotely resembling a contract. His cabinet had given up no secrets, just like his desk. Just like her husband.

She sat on the edge of Gramps's recliner and surveyed Daniel's sanctuary, fighting off the feeling of intrusion—a guilt mixed with the anger still pulsing through her after Daniel hadn't made it to the principal meeting. But she'd been forced into the intrusion, and that was the honest truth.

Then a comment Daniel made when he'd accused her of breaking into Gramps's briefcase wandered through her mind. Why was he so paranoid about that briefcase?

She opened the closet, and there it sat, tumblers scrambled. She squatted in front of the case and placed her thumbs on the clasps. There was no give, and she had no idea what the combination might be. An extra level of intrusion settled on her as she thought about picking the lock.

Under the briefcase was the end of a thin strip of paper, and on it, a single word. *Clarity.* She lifted the case and saw a familiar phrase—*Clarity like you've never experienced before*—next to a logo for Simon's Film Lab and a scrawl she'd seen hundreds of times. It belonged to Daniel.

She picked up the strip with trembling fingers. Between Simon's logo and Daniel's signature was tiny text. She squinted hard.

This represents a sacred contract between the holder and the truth they need to see.

Kelly held in her hand the key to the answers about her husband. His well-being. Her happiness. She raced out of the study, her next stop Simon's to get the photos that upset Daniel so much that he'd flung the last gift from his beloved Gramps to the rocks and pounding surf.

Thirty-Nine

Kelly slid the strip of paper across the counter with a shaky cocktail of fear and trepidation. The whole drive to the film lab had been an infuriating crawl in traffic, with each red light giving her extra time to picture the worst and then wallow in it.

Simon rose on the balls of his feet as he looked down at the counter. "So Daniel has come clean with you."

A lie toyed with her mind. She had to get her hands on Daniel's photos.

Simon smiled into her hesitation. "I'm glad you chose honesty. Your photos will be ready in just a few moments."

The emotion that had threatened to spill over all day lapped again at the edges of her self-control. "I need to know what in these photos is upsetting Daniel so much. He ditched a meeting at school about his daughter's future, and now he isn't returning my calls."

"Truth. Inescapable truth."

"What does that mean?"

Simon stood tall. "Do you remember when you said you were honest with your boss and it hadn't, you said, *worked?* Well, sometimes your honesty doesn't produce results you can see with your eyes. Sometimes the results are about your own integrity. Sometimes they're about the longer term. Sometimes the longest term."

Kelly flashed back to the fleeting adrenaline surge of victory as she strutted from her boss's office at Rubicon Pharma, then forward to now, when her triumph of quitting to his face was crumbling under the erosion of bills and an uncertain future.

Simon stroked his chin and studied her. "Sometimes it takes time. Like with you."

The elation of her win over Arnold ebbed away. "What do you mean?"

Simon gestured to the ornate gold frame on the wall. The tiles in her foyer. Her suitcase now grayed out. On top, the bright purple logo of Beyond Bank. "You've decided not to leave your husband, but the bank account is still open, isn't it? You acknowledge the truth, but still it isn't a part of you."

Kelly dropped her head. "Is that why Daniel won't be honest with me?"

Simon ushered her to the frames. "Honesty doesn't mean telling everything to everyone all the time. Some people take longer to get there than others, like your Gramps. He spent years using the camera to capture the truth in other people's lives before he finally addressed his own. Some people think they can manipulate the

273

world so they can bury the truth or hide from it, but that doesn't work either. Like Becky here."

Simon tapped at a frame crafted from flagstones, holding the image of a woman in a pink pencil skirt applying another layer of pancake makeup to an already made-up face. "She's terrified of people seeing the real her, so she goes nowhere without her mask. For her, the price of honesty will be when her husband tires of a marriage to someone who, deep down, she isn't."

The frame next to it showed a young man running from a horde of suited men, anger writ large on their faces. "Or Andy here, whose desire for the shortcuts in life will keep him running from those he cheats. It will cost him everything."

Kelly thought of the bosses at Rubicon who raked in million-dollar bonuses regardless of their performance. They dismissed truth as an impediment to business. "You know that's not always the case."

Simon beamed. "It's *always* the case. Truth isn't invited in. It's treated as an academic argument that can be discarded if it's unsettling. Sometimes the consequences are immediate, sometimes a little more drawn out. Sometimes they aren't felt until the fog of age clouds the mind, blocking everything but regrets, and they follow people to the grave. Or beyond."

Worst-case scenarios from her drive came back to her. "So what consequences will Daniel face?"

Simon brushed the lapels of his white lab coat. "The same as everyone else. A price to pay for mistakes. It may simply be a different life path, perhaps not the one he should take. But ultimately, an unhappy one. An unfulfilled one."

The sound of a soft buzzer drifted from the back of the lab.

"Excuse me. Daniel's—sorry, your—photographs are ready." Simon drifted to the back of the lab and took care in slipping on white gloves. He extracted several photos from the bowels of the film processor and flipped through them, a solemn smile on his lips.

He brought them back to the counter, where Kelly waited with an outstretched hand.

Simon raised a finger and reached under the counter for an envelope before straightening the photos in it. Then he pulled a large roll of stickers from under the counter and removed one to seal the envelope. He held it out, and Kelly took it with a trembling hand. She turned to leave, but Simon had not yet let go.

"Are you ready to see these, Kelly?"

Forty

Daniel leaned against the window of the laundromat to stop the world from spinning. His directionless walk had taken him in meandering but ever-tightening circles around Simon's Film Lab, and he arrived back with one minute of his long hour left to burn. In that moment, the strained faces of couples slinking through his office door for counseling made sense. Facing the truth wasn't an academic exercise or a problem that just needed a solution. And an hour could feel like ten.

The tiny bell jingled, and Daniel made his way to the counter through a thickening cloud of chemicals. The smell of something developing. "I need to know. Who are you?"

Simon rose on the balls of his feet, and a light laugh came from his lips as he tapped his name tag. "I thought we'd been introduced."

"Very funny."

"It's my job to step in—to shine the light on truth, especially for those people who can't—or won't—face it. To encourage people to accept that their secrets are doing them harm and can destroy those around them if they don't face up to them. In a way, I'm a counselor, just like you."

To Daniel's left was the slightest movement, a shimmering on the surface of one framed photo. He stared at it as the color drained from a young man's face as he focused on a computer screen. One minute the photo was in full vibrancy; the next minute it was gray. Like the photos in Gramps's album.

Simon clapped his hands like a child on Christmas morning. "He's done it." The photo dissolved, leaving the frame empty, as Simon turned to face Daniel. "These other people still think they can outlast the symptoms of their secrets."

Daniel looked down the wall of frames. So many faces. At its end, *No Secrets* still sat in its thick pine frame. Still without his name.

"How did you get these photos?"

"The same way the camera does. Daniel, the truth will win out. It always does. Even for those people who think they can keep their secrets buried, they know they're there, and they suffer because of that knowledge. For some it's an extra burden; they carry it as baggage. Others pretend they're happy with the life they now lead, but deep down they're not. So while they think they've won, they're the ones who later in life sit back and realize just how much they've lost."

Daniel's glance back at Simon crashed into his question. "Is that who you will be, Daniel?"

Daniel dropped his head. "What do I do?"

Simon stood tall. "You need to confess your truth, come clean with those around you, and work hard to win back their trust."

"I can't stop it, can I?"

"Now that you've seen the consequences, why would you want to?"

"My career will be over—so will my marriage. There's no way Kelly will accept that the photo with Anna at the work dinner isn't real."

Simon leaned across the counter with a conspiratorial whisper. "You'd be surprised. And isn't the old saying 'The truth shall set you free'? Maybe you can use your experience of coming clean to help others."

Daniel sat back on his heels. Maybe he could. A tiny spark flickered into life deep within him. The spark of something new. Productive. Meaningful.

Simon's unblinking gaze bored into him. "If you're wavering, the price of not coming clean is something I can show you."

Daniel steeled himself. "I'm ready."

Simon rose on the balls of his feet. "The evidence is in your photos, but I'm afraid they aren't here."

"What?"

"They've already been picked up."

Daniel clutched at the counter as the room started to spin. Who knew about Simon except—

Oh no.

Forty-One

The polished gravel of Daniel's driveway scattered in every direction as he skidded toward his house. He sprinted up the steps and placed a hand on the front door as he analyzed his options.

Apology, seeking mercy.

Confrontation, seeking justification.

Pleading, seeking assurance.

The door swung open to a quiet home. Daniel expected to face either an angry Kelly—hands on hips, ready to deliver an angry salvo—or a distraught Kelly propped up by the kitchen counter.

He saw neither.

Kelly lay on the sofa in silence, her cheeks wet with tears, the photo envelope discarded on the coffee table. The photographs trembled in her hand.

Daniel selected pleading as he rushed to the end of the sofa. "I can explain."

Kelly bolted upright. "Where have you been? I had to face an angry principal on my own!"

The appointment had slipped his mind completely. "I'm so sorry, Kel. I've been dealing with a few things—"

Kelly's face flushed beneath the tears, her anger pulsing through her. "Dealing with a few things? Your daughter has been saying at school that she needs to do something to get our attention, and they might kick her out of St. Arcadia's. I've managed to talk to her, but she won't get help until we get help. And you won't get help because you're protecting your precious career."

Daniel absorbed the body blows. Justification gave way to acceptance of something self-inflicted. And in that moment he knew what he had to do.

More tears flushed away her seething anger. "And if we don't, this is our future!" She thrust the photographs out to him.

With a nervous deep breath, Daniel took them, expecting the worst, the tiniest part of him hoping for the best.

He got the worst.

The first photo showed an unfamiliar reception area for a business. A group photo on the wall hung next to a different Crossroads Counseling logo than the one he'd taken great pride in signing off from the designer. The photo was a snapshot of only three people, not the proud group that had celebrated on the deck of Daniel's cliff-top home.

Another photo. Daniel sat hunched in Gramps's burgundy recliner in a tiny flat, the claustrophobic walls within touching distance of his chair.

Another photo. Kelly sat at an unfamiliar kitchen table set for dinner. For one. Glaring at the ceiling, the sheen of tears on her cheeks.

Daniel flicked to the next image. Kelly read a sheet of paper at this small kitchen table. The purple bank logo bled through the paper.

Daniel flipped through the photographs of his future. Photo after photo—downcast glances, distant eyes, lips set against an unhappy present. He and Kelly miserable. And each alone.

Alone.

It dawned on him. In all these photographs, it wasn't just that they were without each other; they were without someone else.

Milly.

Daniel slumped against the sofa under the weight of unrealized grief at a loss he had not even experienced. Yet.

Kelly sat up, the back of her hand wiping away tears. "This is our future if we don't address our problems. We need to deal with them, because if this is our future, then I've already left and Milly is gone. Forget your career or the dream house. If we don't do something, it will cost us our daughter."

Daniel reeled at the sense of impending discovery, panicked at having the edges of his buried secrets greeted by the light.

Kelly nodded to the photos in Daniel's trembling hand. "I'm happy to talk about what

I need to do, like close the bank account, but I need to know you're happy to keep no secrets as well. And without it turning into a counseling session. Every time I've tried to talk to my husband, I get diagnosed. You try to fix me with your professional hat on. I know why you do it— you like to fix things, and you're so good at it."

Daniel felt his soul puddle into his shoes. His strength at work was a blind spot at home. His advice to Joe and Joanne Average sitting on his couch was simple, but he never followed it. His advice echoed back to him, annoying him with not just its simplicity but the fact that he knew he'd offered it a thousand times without listening to it himself. *You need to bring some things out into the open. You each hold a part of the solution.*

Kelly was on a roll—a cork had popped on emotions long bottled up. "I didn't believe you when you said there was no one else."

"I'd run out of ways to convince you, but that's not—"

"I spoke to Anna, and she has reassured me that there isn't."

The advice pecked away at him again. *You need to bring some things out into the open.*

"I didn't do anything, but it's a little more layered than that, Kel. The group photo on our deck showed me and Anna holding hands."

Pure fear burned in Kelly's stare. Daniel had

seen that look in a woman's eyes countless times when her partner had just announced he had something to say. "But Anna told me—"

"Nothing happened, but the camera showed my heart. I've been relying on her in the way I should have been relying on you."

Silence. A gentle breeze wafted in from the deck. The fear in Kelly's eyes subsided.

"So I'm sorry. I was angry you didn't believe I'd done nothing wrong, but Simon was clear that I wasn't being honest with you in how I viewed Anna." Again, advice he'd doled out for everyone else to follow.

"But if you aren't seeing someone else, why have you been coming home so late?"

"I need to come clean with you about the next book."

Kelly frowned in confusion. "What's wrong with the book?"

"I'm nearly a year behind. It's not happening."

Kelly sat back, stunned. "Not happening? You said you were working on it."

"I've been trying to make it happen, to come up with something, but it just wasn't coming."

Kelly's frown graduated into a scowl. "So when you told me to just wait a few more months—"

"I was genuine in that."

"Why couldn't you tell me? I stayed at my job because I thought the book wasn't far away. Was it just that you were too proud to tell me that the bestselling author couldn't write another book?"

Daniel stared at his feet. He'd kept this secret close for years, convincing himself it would never come out. But now it was about to be brought into the light, halving its power but doubling its risk. "That's what I need to be honest with you about."

The breeze picked up as it drifted through the doors and ruffled Kelly's hair. She leaned back into the couch as partners often did in his counseling sessions. Putting distance between them and whatever was about to be revealed.

Daniel took a deep breath, closed his eyes, and lifted a lid he'd thought was nailed down forever. "The original version of *No Secrets* wasn't mine. It was Howard's."

Kelly blinked hard as her mouth dropped open.

"I found it in his desk when I was cleaning it out after the funeral. I had a big problem—the bank was going to shut down the practice—and I found what I thought was a solution. I told myself it would be okay because I edited most of it. But the lie grew larger every time someone asked me about my inspiration for the book." His words tumbled out like boiling white-water, spilling over one another in a rush to be heard.

Kelly's voice was thin. "Why didn't you tell me?"

"Shame, pride, the fact I thought I could fix

my problems myself. But it's been impossible to come up with an idea for the second book because I didn't come up with the idea for the first."

Kelly flushed beet red. Then she hurried to the kitchen, and with the tap gushing, she filled, then overfilled, a water glass.

"Kelly?"

Kelly drained the glass, and then she filled and overfilled it once more before slamming the tap off. The glass trembled in her hands. "So you're saying that even after working longer than I was supposed to at a job that was destroying me, we'll lose the house?"

Daniel stood, his hands spread wide, his gaze down. A beaten man, but one whose beating left bruises on her as well. "I don't know."

Another gust of wind plucked at their curtains. Kelly's eyes flicked around the room but landed nowhere near Daniel. The loss of respect he'd expected had started its erosion.

Daniel glanced at the photos in his hand. "I didn't want to own up to this with you. More to the point, I didn't want to own up to it with myself. Something in me didn't want you to see me for what I'd done."

"But you've done it, and now I have to pay for it too."

"Fair enough. But it's bigger than that. If that fact about *No Secrets* gets out, I'll be destroyed professionally. If that ever came out in a counseling session in someone else's practice—"

Kelly gestured to the photos. "So what do we do? This is our future if we don't do something about it."

"It's also more than just the two of us. Milly isn't in any of these photos."

"I know." Her tears welled again.

"As much as we have to do this for each other, we have to do it for her. Gramps's camera gave us a chance to do something now, by giving us a glimpse of the future if we don't."

"But you hurled it from the deck. And you threw any benefit to us away with it."

There was no way Daniel could explain his next statement. "The camera is back. I don't know how, but it's back. And it's intact." He studied her expression—he would have to bring out the camera to prove it.

Instead, a light laugh escaped from Kelly. "I'm not really surprised. Simon said the photos were magical."

Daniel's cogs whirred at this unexpected response. "So I can't get rid of the camera, but I need to get rid of the secrets. And that means we could lose the house."

Kelly brushed away the first of what he knew would be many tears yet to come. Then she gave him a slow nod, the gradual acceptance of the inevitable.

"You were right, Kelly, and the solution needs to start with all three of us seeing someone. That way Milly isn't wondering if we're working through our problems. She'll be a part of the conversation."

"But what if the story about Howard's book gets out?"

Daniel bowed his head. "I'll deal with it then."

Wind billowed their curtains, and Kelly moved to shut the doors to the deck. Her eyes widened as her hand covered her mouth. A single screamed word forced its way out between her fingers.

"Milly!" She threw open the doors.

Through the window, Daniel could see Milly, arms out, her jazz shoes wobbling on the railing.

And she was crying.

Forty-Two

Daniel rushed through the open doors, his princess half an inch from losing her footing, wobbling in the buffeting wind, about to head toward the path Gramps's camera followed as it plummeted to the rocks two hundred feet below.

Kelly's already thin voice strained into the wind. "Milly, please get down."

"I don't want to be that kid with two homes who has to work out which parent I'm with each Saturday."

Daniel took a cautious step forward, his hands outstretched. "Step down, and then we'll talk."

Milly's arms waved as another gust tipped her balance. "I don't want to talk like you want to talk, when you try to fix me instead of listening." Her words sliced deep into Daniel's heart.

"Okay. Then let's trade questions, but first you have to get down from there." He took another step toward her.

Milly's arms windmilled, a mixture of fear and determination washing across her face. But she righted herself. "If I can ask the first question."

Daniel eased forward another step, the wind swirling around him. "I want you to know Mom and I have agreed to talk to someone together, and we'd like you to come with us. You can ask all the questions you want."

Kelly stepped forward. "But we need you to come down."

Another gust of wind battered her, and a foot slipped over the railing. Milly screamed as she bent, thrusting out two hands as Daniel and Kelly leaped forward, each taking one. A split second after her jazz shoes hit the deck, she buried her face between them.

Daniel breathed again as he clutched his daughter.

Milly pulled away and leaned against the railing, her chest heaving, her brows knitting again. "I want the first question."

Daniel started to fold his arms before thinking better of it. He left them hanging at his sides. "Okay, shoot."

"Did you just come out here because I looked like I was going to jump?"

Kelly rushed to wrap her in an embrace. "Of course, sweetie. I didn't want you to fall."

Daniel studied his only child, the father and counselor within him jostling for position. Her question was deeper than that. "No, we needed to tell you we're going to talk to someone. You standing on the railing just made it happen faster."

Milly nodded, and the first smile in months threatened to creep across her face.

Daniel thrust his hands into his pockets. "My turn. What would you have done if we hadn't come out?"

Kelly squatted in front of Milly, hands on her shoulders, as if giving her space to answer without letting go. "I don't know, but the only time you two talk about anything is when it's about me, so I had to do something."

"But what if it got so windy—"

Milly shushed him with a finger. "My turn. What made you and Mom decide to talk to someone?"

Kelly turned to Daniel as if expectantly waiting for his answer. This was going to sound crazy, but he had to say it. "Gramps's camera. It showed me truth about my life, and that I haven't been following my own advice. I tell everyone else to keep no secrets, but I haven't done that with you. Or with Mom. I need to say I'm sorry—to both of you."

Milly nodded. "That explains what Gramps told me."

Daniel's quick glance at Kelly collided with the one she shot him.

"He kept telling me the camera never lies. That's why I've been taking photos of you, because I was trying to find out what was really going on—seeing as you never told me. But it never showed me anything, so I'm not sure if I believe him anymore."

That explained her photos. She was looking for truth the whole time, and when she didn't find it, she created it. With camera angles and overlaid hot-pink love hearts.

Kelly stood and held Milly tight. "Is it my turn to ask a question?"

Milly nodded, her cheeks tugging with her emerging smile.

"With your school grades, was that all just to get our attention?"

Milly's smile faltered, her quick eyes darting to Daniel's face. "Um, yes."

So there was more behind her performance at school. Thank goodness Anna had made a connection with her.

Kelly hugged Milly tighter. "Thanks for being honest with me. Can I ask one more question?"

"Sure," Daniel and Milly answered in unison.

"Can we go inside? It's freezing out here."

Forty-Three

Daniel took a deep breath as he stood outside Anna's open office door. He had to start with her. She deserved it.

At his polite knock, Anna looked up from her laptop and smiled. "You look better than the last time I saw you."

"Things are on the up."

Anna nodded. Professionally.

"I need to come clean with you." He closed the door behind him.

"Okay." She gestured to her couch and tapped her fingers together under her chin.

There was no other way to say it. "*No Secrets* was first written by Howard."

Anna's fingers froze mid-tap.

"When we were cleaning out his office after the funeral, I found the manuscript in his desk. I rewrote some of it, but it's pretty much his."

Anna's eyebrow stayed low, but her mouth dropped open in shock. "You stole Howard's book?" She retreated into professional silence.

"Yes." He studied her.

Tears formed in Anna's eyes. "How could you?"

Daniel knee-jerked into defense to justify what

he'd done. After all, he'd saved the practice. But then he quickly thought better of it. "At the time it solved the problem of the bank wanting to shut us down, but that doesn't change the fact that the book was Howard's."

"It's not fraud, is it?"

Daniel shrugged. "I don't know. I've left a message with the publisher."

Anna nodded, lips pursed, her eyes flicking around the room. "Well, even if it is, I'll stand by you, as a professional and as a friend."

Daniel was touched. "Thank you, and there's something else." The vertigo again pooled at the base of his spine as another uncomfortable revelation was about to be breathed into life. "Do you remember when we talked about Kelly thinking there was someone else? You asked me if I'd given her any reason to think there was. Well, I've been thinking about you inappropriately."

Anna flushed. "Daniel!"

"No, not like that, but I've been relying on you more than I should be. More than on Kelly."

Anna raised an eyebrow. That eyebrow. "So that's why Kelly thought there was something between us?"

"There was also Monique. I could say Kelly was threatened by her—and she probably was—but I need to own my behavior. I might have been leading her on, and that wasn't the right thing to do."

"Monique needs to hear that." She buzzed reception on her desk phone. "Do you have a moment?"

Monique trudged into Anna's office, her usual bounce gone, her lips a dull shade of purple. "Yes?"

Her transformation shocked him. Was he responsible for this as well? He rubbed his hands and caught her eye. "Monique, I flirted with you, and I'm sorry. I meant what I said to you. You don't need the attention of other people to justify being alive. You're a great young woman who doesn't need other people's approval."

She burst into a shower of tears.

"I mentioned to you before that your *friend* could have a more professional conversation. Would you like that?"

Monique bowed her head, a mumble coming from her chest. "You've got no idea how hard it is to work in a place where everyone else has it together. To be happy all the time when you're broken inside."

Actually, I do.

Anna leaned forward, offering Monique a tissue. "You'd be surprised just how many people feel that."

The sense of vertigo was back. "Me included."

Monique's head snapped up to look at him. "Really?"

Daniel held back a laugh as Gramps's wisdom

again rang true. "There's more to life than what we see. We all struggle with our own acceptance of truth, especially when it points to something we would prefer not to see."

"Maybe you should put that in your next book."

The spark within him flicked into flame. His next book. Maybe it was closer than he realized.

The phone out in the reception area rang, and Monique touched her Bluetooth headset as she gathered her composure. "Welcome to Crossroads Counseling. This is Monique."

She nodded and shot another look at Daniel, her lips giving him a silent warning. *Your editor.*

Daniel took a deep breath. This was the call that could either save him or cost him everything. He hurried to his office to take it, steeled himself, and pressed the flashing red button. "Amanda!"

"Returning your call, Daniel." Amanda's voice was flat. Very flat.

A wash of anxiety covered Daniel in its usual anesthetic wave, but it was tinged with something different. Something almost justified. Something earned.

Daniel took a deep breath and closed his eyes.

Forty-Four

The reflections of Daniel's family stared back at him from the polished front window of Simon's Film Lab. It had been a roller-coaster twenty-four hours since Milly stepped down from the railing. A reawakening of connection. A realization of a now uncertain future. But certainty in facing it together.

"How about we get some dumplings after we've seen Simon?" It felt right to start the next phase of life with a celebration. They might be the last dumplings they had for a while.

The little bell jingled as Kelly stepped past Daniel and the wall full of frames opposite the shelves of cameras. She enveloped Simon in a hug when he stepped out from behind the counter.

"It's wonderful to see you, too, Kelly."

"I've got something to show you." She reached into her handbag and pulled out a sheet of paper bearing a bright purple logo. "I closed it." She tore the bank statement in two and threw both halves into the air.

Tears glistened in Simon's eyes. "You've accepted your truth. Now you're on a happier path." To Kelly's left, the slightest movement—the fluttering of butterfly wings. In the ornate gold frame, the bright purple sitting on top of her now-grayed suitcase drained of color before the entire picture dematerialized, leaving just a blank sheet of glossy white paper.

Daniel strode to a large pine frame at the far end of the wall. He stood before it as the front cover of his book evaporated. Relief washed over him as his secret was replaced by a curly-headed young man hurling a remote control at a basketball game on TV, a fierce desperation in his eyes.

Simon wiped the tears from his cheeks. "I'm so proud of both of you. Where is Gramps's camera, Daniel?"

"It's on my desk at home, and it's taken no more photos."

"Perhaps the camera has revealed its truth for you. Maybe you need to give it to someone who needs it as much as you did."

He smiled at Kelly. They'd discussed that very thing an hour earlier.

"I must admit, I did toy again with the idea of using the camera in my counseling sessions, thinking it could help me cut to the chase with those people who sit in front of me in flat-out denial."

"And how did that work out when you tried it?"

"It's just disappointing not being able to use such a powerful tool to help people be honest with themselves."

"Well, Daniel, even when you were faced with the truth, your life turned around only when you accepted it. When you decided to come clean with those around you."

A low-burning flame within him that had started with the tiniest spark flared into life, fanned by his imagination. He could share his story of hiding secrets and working through the process of revealing them.

On paper.

In book two.

Daniel felt light-headed with relief as the story unfolded in his head, but the risk loomed large. Difficult, and out of his control. Coming clean with Kelly, Milly, work, his publisher . . . Doubt dripped onto one corner of his burgeoning resolve as he realized how hard he would have to work to win back their trust. And without a guarantee that the effort would work.

Daniel stepped closer to him. "May I tell the story of your film lab and the cameras you sell in my next book?"

Simon bowed. "If you like."

"It would be a powerful accompaniment to how my life turned around when I had no option but to focus on the truth."

Kelly stared at Simon. "Where did you come from?"

"The question you *should* ask is, where am I needed next?"

Daniel chuckled. He shouldn't have expected anything different from this strange young man. "Thanks so much for showing us what we needed to see. You saved us."

Simon looked past them to the girl standing just inside the doorway—without earbuds. He rushed to greet her with an outstretched hand. "It's Milly, isn't it? It is an absolute pleasure to meet you. Gosh, you remind me of your father."

Milly winced amid an awkward handshake. Daniel smiled at his daughter. She had become so much happier in one day.

Milly seemed to be sizing Simon up as she withdrew her hand. "Are you the guy who did something to make Mom and Dad patch things up?"

Simon nodded, once.

"Well, thanks . . . for whatever you did."

Simon smiled. "You should thank your parents. They brought their problems out into the open. They each held a part of the solution." He winked at Daniel. "All I did was comfort them in the knowledge that the truth—one of the most powerful forces in life—would set them free."

"So long, Simon." Daniel bid him farewell with a firm handshake. "I'll make sure I tell others to come and see you—with or without cameras and film—or at least remind them there's truly more to life than what they see."

Simon bit his lower lip, his eyes again

glistening. "Your next book will be more than reminding others of the truth around them. It will also be about accepting truth yourself. You may find the person who needs this book the most is you."

Kelly hugged Simon again, and the tiny bell jingled their departure from the film lab.

The red-and-yellow paper lanterns fluttered as Kelly stepped into Ming's Court Chinese Restaurant. The proprietor came to meet them, reaching out to hold Kelly's hands.

"Welcome, welcome! So pleased to see you again, Daniel, and this time you have brought your family!" He bowed slightly to Milly. "And your daughter has grown so much."

Milly smiled back at him. Another smile, so soon after the first. It was so good to see.

Mr. Ming flitted around them, scanning the empty room for a free table. "Please, please, I will find a table for you."

A thought jumped up at Kelly. "Oh no! I left that bank statement behind. It's better if I dispose of it. I don't want my personal information out there for anyone to see. I'll only be a minute."

Kelly hurried past the bubbling fish tank, and the paper lanterns swung hard in her wake as she stepped outside. Her phone pinged. A text. From Jasmine. "Hey, check out the news tonight. I think you might have left Rubicon Pharma at just the right time. Tarquin was just marched out of the building."

Smiling to herself, Kelly leaned on the door to Simon's Film Lab, but there was no jingle. She looked up in surprise. The shop that was bright and welcoming a minute ago was now dark. Dust and cobwebs covered the window, and when she peered through, she saw no frames on the wall. No cameras on shelves. The glass counter was dusty as well, and in the faint light, she could see that the back of the film lab was empty.

And under her hand, a For Lease sign had been stuck on the middle of the door.

Forty-Five

As if to catch its breath, the blinking cursor screeched to a halt on Daniel's screen. Then it resumed its scooting, chased by rapid-fire letters bursting from Daniel's flashing fingers. He flicked a glance at Gramps's open briefcase, now sitting on his home office desk.

Chapter after chapter of *Coming Clean* poured out of him at a rate of a thousand words an hour. And good words, not just verbiage that the cold light of a new day would slash and burn. He would be finished with his first draft today, and he just knew he could find another publisher. He had to. Amanda's email was surgical and precise in its wording, as most emails drafted by a legal team are. They were looking at their options. Legal ones.

Each glance at the camera and album, which leaned against the worn and faded paisley pattern, revealed another inspiration as he added to his grandfather's story. It was no longer just a journey of eighty-eight years; it now had an extra three weeks tacked onto the end, which even on their own felt like nearly nine decades.

A rising confidence he could pull this off overshadowed the usual numbing anxiety. He *had* to find a publisher. *Coming Clean* would not only have a powerful message about honesty but also an author living the consequences of keeping secrets in real time.

Daniel's fingers flashed faster as the words continued to fly, telling how he'd accepted the fact that truth could be more a journey than a destination. How he'd accepted that challenge for himself, for those he worked with, and for those his experience had touched.

No chapter held back. As each of his failings presented itself for examination, he felt as if three years of stress peeled away like sunburned skin, revealing a fresh, vibrant layer beneath. Simon was right. The chief beneficiary of this book was him.

His fingers slowed as he approached the end of another chapter and the current point in his life. His index finger tapped at the keys. He couldn't end the story here. Something was missing.

Daniel leaned across to the briefcase and picked up the photo album, the cardboard groaning as he flicked through its pages. His eyes were now open to the truth held under tiny black triangles. These photos didn't show just the worst of the people in them; they were their truest representation. These weren't people before the right moment; they were people right in the moment, or the consequence of it. Garth could have been homeless had he not addressed his drinking. Gramps's other friends could have been destroyed had they followed their addictions. His own marriage could have been over.

Daniel laid the album back in the briefcase and pulled out the camera. The tiny window on top of it still read "1." As it had from the moment they'd gone to counseling.

Daniel sighed. It *would* be so handy to have this camera in his office at Crossroads. But being confronted with truth was one thing; dealing with it was another. He placed the camera back in the briefcase, almost with reverence. He had been saved from a broken and lonely future. And he knew what needed to happen with the camera now.

Daniel pulled the envelope with familiar upright writing on it from the briefcase. He opened the letter inside and read it again. When he propped it up on a photo of Kelly, Milly, and himself, he knew how he would complete the book. At the beginning.

He closed his eyes for a moment. Then he scrolled back to the start of the document, and with a gentle sigh, his fingers moved almost of their own accord.

Gramps, very little surprises me, but the gift of your camera did. It helped me see beyond the knowledge I thought I had, to see that sometimes the best way to come clean is to acknowledge that the peace of truth outweighs the pain of revelation.

You were right to worry about my family. I shifted the conversation away every time you tried to talk to me about what was going on because it was another reminder of my failure. I was less than the person I wanted you to see, than the person I wanted to be. Without the camera I wouldn't have lasted. I thought I could work through my problems on my own, but I couldn't. I needed the ability to hide my secrets taken away.

So thanks for your gift. I'm so sorry I couldn't have helped you overcome your demons, but I'm forever proud that you did.

Now I talk with my clients differently. The camera has taught me there's always more to life than what we see, and I truly believe it.

Tears streamed down Daniel's face.

I love you, Gramps.
Daniel

He stared at the blinking cursor. The book was complete. He folded Gramps's letter and returned it to its envelope, and then his eyes settled on the family photo on which it had rested. His mother had taken it after their first counseling session. They were sitting on their sofa, the sun flooding over them from the deck. Milly beamed from between her parents, Daniel's arm around her shoulder and resting on Kelly's. Renewed hope shone in three pairs of eyes—a hope not clouded by an uncertain future but ready to take it on.

Epilogue

The music drifted from Milly's bookshelf, filling her room instead of being pumped into her ears. She turned the tiny canister over, its metal cold in her fingers, a foreign object to someone whose photos appeared in her hand in an instant.

Life had been better the past two weeks than for as long as she could remember. The low cloud that seemed to hang over every conversation had lifted, and Mom and Dad were trying, which was all she'd ever wanted.

It was all because of Gramps's camera. Dad had said as much when he gave it to her, telling her it had saved him. But he didn't say how. She needed to know.

She studied the numbers on the film canister: ISO 400, whatever that meant. Twenty-four. The number of photos you could take. She'd taken five or six photos of Mom and Dad, but now the little red F on the camera told her the film was full. Dad couldn't help himself—maybe that was why he'd given her a whole box of film.

Anyway, this tiny tube of metal held twenty-four photos, but Simon's shop was closed. Who would turn the film into photos now? Dad said

Monique found only one place in the whole city.

Milly put the canister on her bedside table and grabbed her tablet. She swiped away the news update—something about the drug company Mom used to work for and a government investigation—and fired up Google.

Film . . . photos . . . laboratory . . .

The first search result popped onto her screen, and Milly laughed.

Simon's Film Lab.

So much for Dad saying the guy was gone. His shop was just online, like every shop was. She touched her way through to the website. Yes, that was him. A smiling man with slicked-back silver hair, a white lab coat, and a red-and-yellow name badge. A handmade font scrawled across his image: *Clarity like you've never experienced before!*

Milly stared at him. Strange-looking guy. Young but old, and he had a twinkle in his eye. That had to be a filter.

A link at the top of the screen pulsed and glowed. *Cameras.* Milly opened the page and flicked her way past thick black cameras. Others were wooden and boxy. Nothing exciting . . . plus, she already had an old camera. Why would she need another one? What she needed was someone to turn her film into photos.

A second link pulsed and glowed. *Gallery.* She

flicked her way down a page filled with faces. The photos were embarrassing. No smiles, no good angles. Someone even looked like they didn't want to get caught eating a whole block of chocolate. It was almost as if people didn't know the camera was there. Weird.

Another link at the top of the page pulsed and glowed in yellow text. *Send us your film!*

Milly's finger hovered over it as a chat window popped up with a ping and a text pulsed in bright red.

Someone is typing . . .

Another ping, and a message flashed into the bottom corner of her screen.

Welcome to Simon's Film Lab! How may I help you today?

A Note from the Author

Dear Friend,

Thank you for investing your time in reading *The Camera Never Lies*. I hope you enjoyed the story and the message woven through it.

And I hope you had more fun reading it than I had writing it.

No, this isn't a confession, where you learn that the original idea for *The Camera Never Lies* was found in the desk of my mentor after he died. The book concept is mine. Honestly. And my mentor is still alive. I think. I should call him.

The challenge I found when writing this book is that it started as the story of a marriage counselor and addressed the question, What would it look like if a man's secrets were revealed to those around him? But then the story became a story not of a marriage counselor but of a marriage, and that's where the challenge began. Again, this is not a confession, but more a realization that our honesty (or rejection of it) comes with messy consequences. And those consequences are often felt by others. In Daniel's case, by his wife and daughter. In Kelly's case, by her husband and daughter. Poor Milly.

The more I explored the secrets Daniel and

Kelly held from each other, the clearer it became that turning your back on something that's an inalienable truth is more than a rejection of honesty. It's a choice that comes packed with a punch, and even if you duck the blow, it can hit others.

My stories always come with a theme. With *The Baggage Handler*, the story was about dealing with emotional baggage. With *The Camera Never Lies*, the theme is about the price of accepting honesty with others and ourselves.

I'd like to ask you a question. How did you respond when Daniel or Kelly looked to take a shortcut or a step in the wrong direction to preserve a lie or to keep the truth hidden for slightly longer?

Remember your response, because it's important. That response was your own response to truth. It can be much easier to see it in someone else's life. I know it is for me, and it may be the case for you as well.

It certainly was for a hotshot marriage counselor with a bestselling book.

So what do you do when you're faced with both the path of truth and another path? Do you decide to face the truth in your life? Or do you weigh the consequences of your preferred path to see if it's worth it—the pain of revelation outweighing the peace of truth?

These are age-old questions. The answers

might not be easy to hear, but that doesn't mean the questions aren't worth asking. If you'd like to explore this further, I have some starter questions on the next page. It isn't homework—think of it more like flicking through a series of photos and finding a deeper truth within them.

Take care,
David

Discussion Questions

1. What power do secrets hold over people, and why do so many people choose to keep their secrets hidden?
2. How did you respond when Daniel or Kelly looked to take a shortcut or a step in the wrong direction to preserve a lie or keep the truth hidden for slightly longer?
3. Simon sometimes held on to the envelopes with Daniel or Kelly's photos for a little too long. What do you think is the significance of that?
4. Do you have friends or family who are carrying a secret they should perhaps deal with? If so, how can you best support them in dealing with it?
5. Why do people hide from the truth they try to keep secret?
6. What do you do when you're faced with truth and another path? Do you weigh the consequences of your preferred path to see if it's worth it? Or do you decide to face the truth in life?
7. What is the one secret you hold that would devastate you the most if a camera mysteriously revealed it to those around

you? What is that secret doing to your future, and what is it doing to your present?

8. If you were given a camera that revealed secrets, would you be tempted to use it to uncover other people's secrets like Daniel was tempted?

9. Which person (or people or group) would be the first you'd take photos of? Should you perhaps deal with anything in your answer, even if you're camera-less?

10. Reflect on Simon's statement:

"Daniel, the truth will win out. It always does. Even for those people who think they can keep their secrets buried, they know they're there, and they suffer because of that knowledge. For some it's an extra burden; they carry it as baggage. Others pretend they're happy with the life they now lead, but deep down they're not. So while they think they've won, they're the ones who later in life sit back and realize just how much they've lost."

Is that true for the people around you? Is it true for you?

11. Should some secrets never be revealed? Why?

12. What do you think *will* happen to Daniel in terms of the consequences of his secrets?
13. What do you think *should* happen? Does what you think *should* happen differ from what you think *will* happen? If so, why?

Acknowledgments

To God: Thank you for making this possible, in so many ways.

To my family: Nicky, Cameron, Daniella, and Emily, thank you for your patience in hearing about magical cameras and secrets—with a special shout-out to Emily, my little beta reader and finder of typos.

To the team behind me: James L. Rubart, it means a lot when authors you look up to hear your concept for a book and love it as much as you do; Steve Laube, whose wise counsel in short email bursts is greatly appreciated; my parents, thank you for your unwavering enthusiasm for the little wins; and the Fulwood family, my first fans ☺.

To the team at HarperCollins Christian Publishing: Becky Monds (for being the best editorial director ever), Paul Fisher, Allison Carter, Laura Wheeler, Savannah Summers, Kevin Hyer, and Kristen Ingebretson. Your partnership across the ocean, a dozen time zones, and several cultures means a lot. I appreciate each one of you for the work you do to bring a story from inside my head to the outside world. And to Jean Bloom, for her line editor's eagle eye and translation skills to assist with my mother tongue of Australian.

To my Debut Authors Group: Jess, Rachel, Melissa, Joy, Tari, Natalie, Abigail, Lauren, and Hannah. It has been a joy to share in the excitement of our first year in publishing. Long may the stories continue!

All characters in this work are fictitious. Resemblance to real persons, living or dead, is purely coincidental, although if you see yourself in these pages, maybe someone's trying to tell you something.

About the Author

David Rawlings is an Australian author, and a sports-mad father of three who loves humor and a clever turn of phrase. Over a twenty-five-year career he has put words on the page to put food on the table, developing from sports journalism and copywriting to corporate communication. Now in fiction, he entices readers to look deeper into life with stories that combine the everyday with a sense of the speculative, addressing the fundamental questions we all face.

Website: www.davidrawlings.com.au
Facebook: David Rawlings – Author
Instagram: davidrawlingsauthor
Twitter: @DavidJRawlings

Books are produced in the United States using U.S.-based materials

Books are printed using a revolutionary new process called THINKtech™ that lowers energy usage by 70% and increases overall quality

Books are durable and flexible because of Smyth-sewing

Paper is sourced using environmentally responsible foresting methods and the paper is acid-free

Center Point Large Print
600 Brooks Road / PO Box 1
Thorndike, ME 04986-0001 USA

(207) 568-3717

US & Canada:
1 800 929-9108
www.centerpointlargeprint.com